U0074166

用對的方法充實自己，
讓人生變得更美好！

臨時需要的一句話！

3秒 用聊天學英文句型就學會

User's Guide 使用說明

英文不好也不怕！
讓這本書成為你聊天的「句型藍圖」，無論是想跟外國人聊聊天、交朋友，都能快速的用英語與世界溝通！

01 超強功能的句型藍圖！
一手掌握好用句型，聊天快速上手

本書編排著重在貼近日常生活的各種情境對話。進入各情境對話前，提供學習者簡單到複雜的句型整理，讓學習者能在開口大聲說英語前，腦海中先有個句型藍圖，英文就能好上手；同時，再勤加開口練習精華句型，英語聊天功力必能大幅增進。

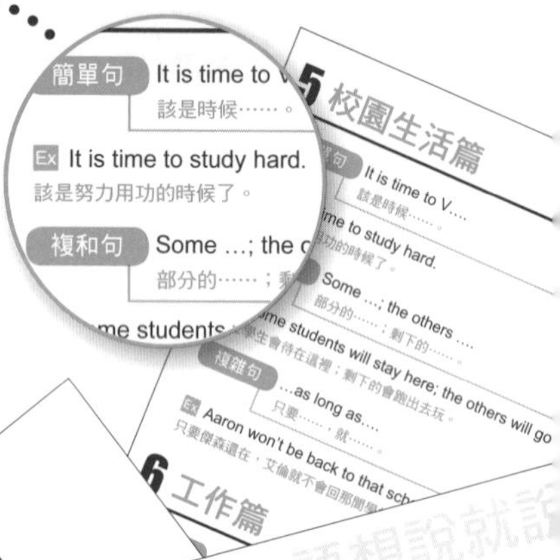
5 校園生活篇
簡單句 It is time to V....
該是時候……。
Ex It is time to study hard.
該是努力用功的時候了。
複和句 Some ...; the others ...
部分的……；剩下的……。
Some students will stay here; the others will go
複雜句 ...as long as....
只要……，就……。
Ex Aaron won't be back to that sch
6 工作篇

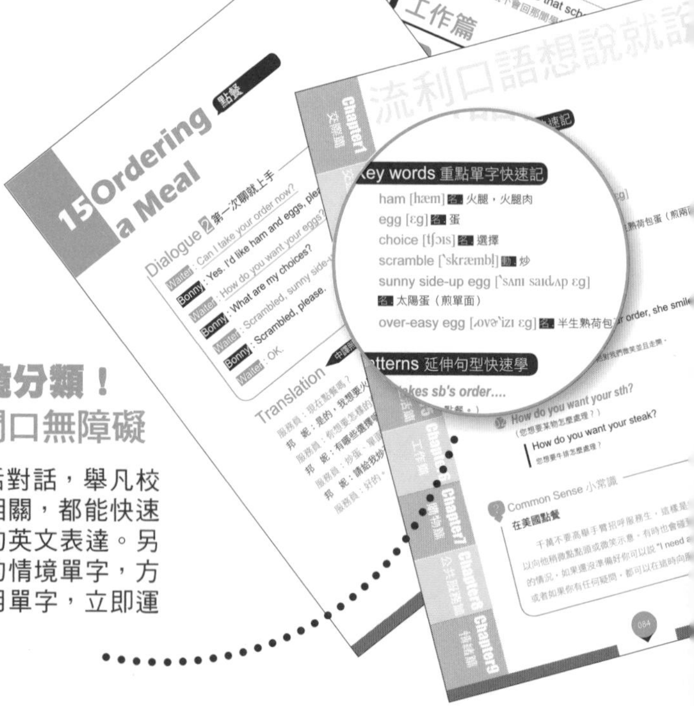
15 Ordering a Meal 點餐
Dialogue 2 第一次聊就上手
Waiter: Can I take your order now?
Bonny: Yes. I'd like ham and eggs, please.
Waiter: How do you want your eggs?
Bonny: What are my choices?
Waiter: Scrambled, sunny side-up...
Bonny: Scrambled, please.
Waiter: OK.
Translation
流利口語想說就說
Key words 重點單字快速記
ham [hæm] 名 火腿，火腿肉
egg [ɛg] 名 蛋
choice [tʃɔɪs] 名 選擇
scramble [ˋskræmbḷ] 動 炒
sunny side-up egg [ˋsʌnɪ saɪd,ʌp ɛg] 名 太陽蛋（煎單面）
over-easy egg [,ovəˋizɪ ɛg] 名 半生熟荷包蛋
Patterns 延伸句型快速學
How do you want your sth?
Common Sense 小常識
在美國點餐

02 豐富生活情境分類！
身歷其境，開口無障礙

本書共含62則生活對話，舉凡校園生活、工作和社交相關，都能快速查找，讓你用最適切的英文表達。另外，貼心選出對話中的情境單字，方便學習者快速掌握常用單字，立即運用。

03 高頻生活句型，快速提升表達力！

關鍵性重點句型&變身句型，延伸學更多

每一單元再延伸兩組常用句型及例句，只要依公式造句，即能再提昇英文表達能力。另外還補充多組的同義相似例句，更能大幅增加句型活用的實力。

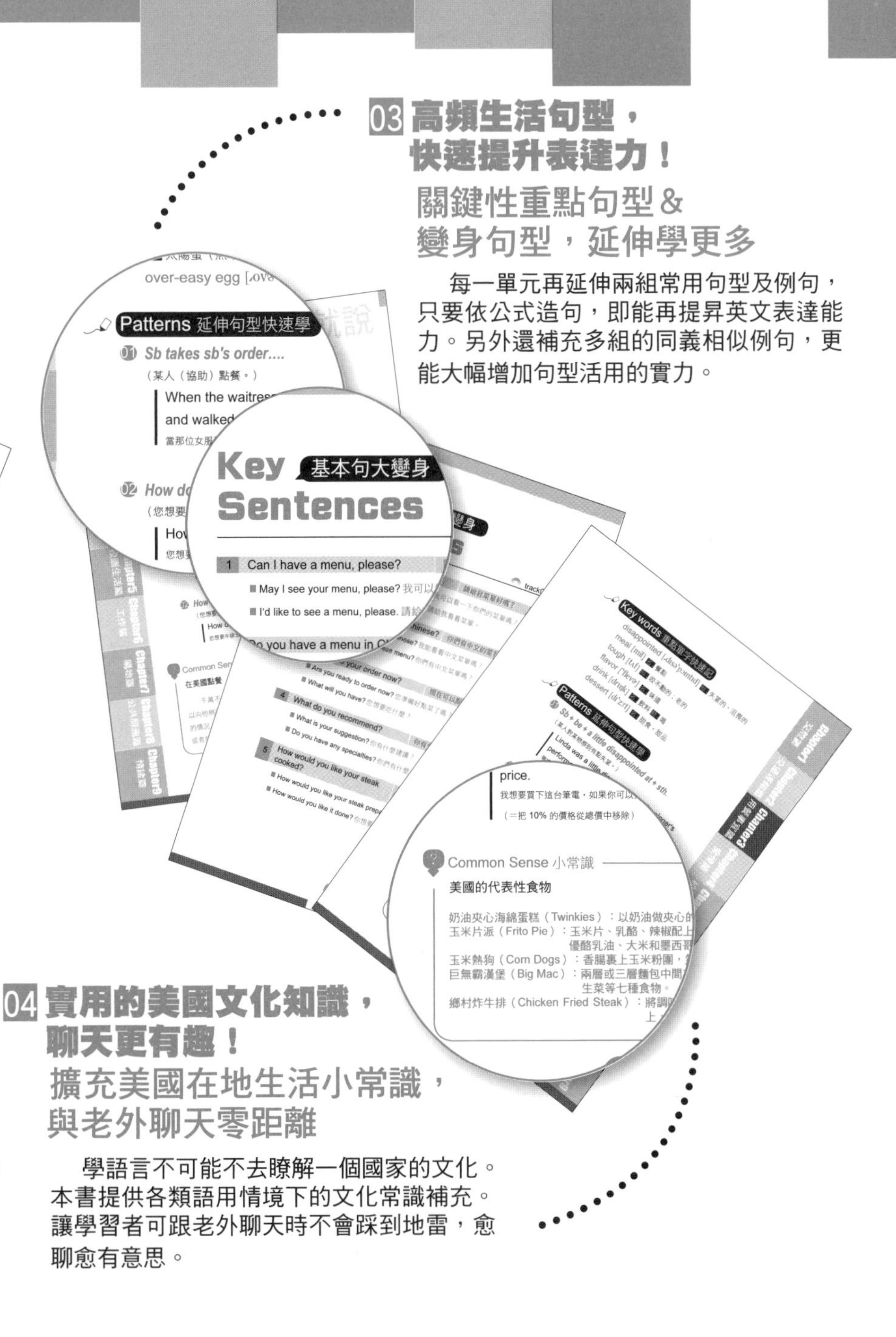

04 實用的美國文化知識，聊天更有趣！

擴充美國在地生活小常識，與老外聊天零距離

學語言不可能不去瞭解一個國家的文化。本書提供各類語用情境下的文化常識補充。讓學習者可跟老外聊天時不會踩到地雷，愈聊愈有意思。

Preface
前言

常常聽到很多人問，學習了那麼多年的英語，但每當遇到需要用英文的時候，卻仍然無法勇敢開口說，到底是為什麼？也許你也有這樣的感嘆。到底英文是不是真的這麼難？學習英語真的就沒有較為簡單有效率的方式了嗎？事實並非如此。本書特別針對常見的主題情境，精心整理出可以在各式情境中聊天應用的好用句型，建立學習者腦中的句庫。當你在真正需要用到英語時，學習者腦中即能馬上浮現句型藍圖，再配合各式情境的常用詞彙，就能依據情境需求，開口說出常用句子，達到基本生活英語的溝通功能。

考慮到要培養學習者對基本生活英語溝通上的掌握度，本書根據教師們普遍認可的「情境式語言學習法」，設計九篇主要情境。情境涵蓋範圍包含校園生活、工作生活，以及社交生活等，希望學習者能活用由淺入深的句型藍圖、重點單字，搭配各類生活情境，以角色扮演的方式，想像自己在該情境下會如何應答，進而熟練常用句型。希望這樣的編排設計能讓讀者活用基本句型單字，有勇氣及足夠的信心開口說英語。

針對讀者更多的需求，我們也整理出最常使用的英語基本句型，輔以變身的基本句。目的是希望擴充學習者腦中的句庫，讓學習者可以學會活用基本句型，使其在相似情境下，說出適合該情境的句子。

此外，本書在每個單元後特別設計有關國外的文化小常識，讓學習者不僅僅只是學到英文的語言形式，更可以深入國外的文化，累積文化觀及語言使用上的背景知識，讓英文能配合實境應用，成為學習者得心應手的溝通工具。

Contents
目錄

Communication 交際篇

Transportation 交通運輸篇

Diet 用餐事宜篇

Contents
目錄

Love 愛情篇

Chapter 5

School Life 校園生活篇

Chapter 6

Work 工作篇

Shopping 購物篇

Public Service 公共服務篇

Feelings 情緒篇

特別企劃

句型藍圖

聊天超好用句型整理

簡單句（含直述句 & 問句）

- 簡單句是表達出一個完整想法的句子。

複和句

- 複和句中使用對等連詞（for, and, nor, but, or, yet, so）或分號連結兩個獨立句子（可表達完整想法，並單獨存在的句子）。

複雜句

- 複雜句為一個獨立子句，再加上至少一個從屬子句（必須跟著獨立子句一起出現的句子）。獨立子句與從屬子句間需要用從屬連接詞（如：after、although、as long as、because、if、since、when 等）連接。

1 交際篇

簡單句 How do you like + N?
你覺得……怎麼樣？

Ex How do you like that movie?
你覺得那部電影怎麼樣？

複和句 …, so …
……，所以……。

Ex Ken loves to help people, so he is quite popular in the chess club.
肯恩喜歡助人，所以他在西洋棋社團中是個很受歡迎的人。

複雜句 If S + V, S + V....
如果……，……。

Ex If you'd like to make friends with her, you'd better have some patience.
如果你想要成為她的朋友，你最好有點耐心。

2 交通運輸篇

簡單句 Can you show me...?
你可以告訴我……嗎？

Ex Can you show me the way to VIESHOW movie theater?
你可以告訴我如何到威秀電影院嗎？

複和句 ...there is no...., and S + V....
沒有任何……，……

Ex There is no excuse to be late, and you should be here before 9 o'clock.
沒有任何理由遲到，你應該九點前就要到了。

複雜句 I'm wondering if you + V....
我在想你是否……。

Ex I'm wondering if you can give the seat to the old man.
我在想你是否願意讓位給這個老人。

3 用餐事宜篇

簡單句 Can you recommend...?
你能推薦……嗎？

Ex Can you recommend me some good food?
你能推薦我一些好吃的食物嗎？

複和句 Sth is …, and it …
某物……，而且……。

Ex The bread is hard, and it tastes bad.
麵包很硬，而且不好吃。

複雜句 S + V (+O) because S + V (+O).
……，因為……。

Ex Jack was happy because the Italian meal satisfied him.
傑克很開心因為義大利餐點讓他很滿意。

4 愛情篇

簡單句 S + have / has a crush + on + ….
某人迷戀……。

Ex Lily has a crush on that movie star.
莉莉迷戀那個電影明星。

複和句 I've tried, but….
我試過了，但……。

Ex I've tried, but she didn't want to listen.
我試過了，但她就是不想聽。

複雜句 S + has/has been + Adj. since S + V…
自從……之後，……。

Ex My brother has been happy since Cindy agreed to marry him.
自從辛蒂答應要嫁給我弟之後，我弟的心情一直很好。

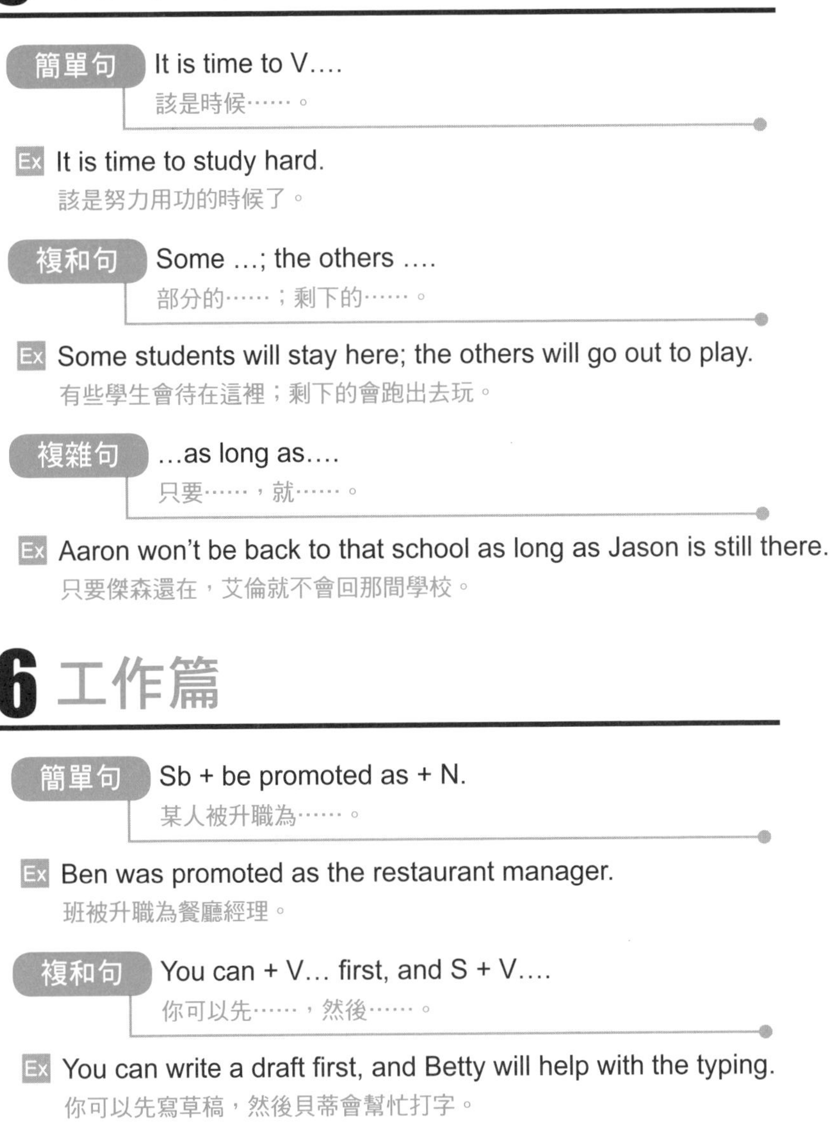

5 校園生活篇

簡單句 It is time to V….

該是時候……。

Ex It is time to study hard.

該是努力用功的時候了。

複和句 Some …; the others ….

部分的……；剩下的……。

Ex Some students will stay here; the others will go out to play.

有些學生會待在這裡；剩下的會跑出去玩。

複雜句 …as long as….

只要……，就……。

Ex Aaron won't be back to that school as long as Jason is still there.

只要傑森還在，艾倫就不會回那間學校。

6 工作篇

簡單句 Sb + be promoted as + N.

某人被升職為……。

Ex Ben was promoted as the restaurant manager.

班被升職為餐廳經理。

複和句 You can + V… first, and S + V….

你可以先……，然後……。

Ex You can write a draft first, and Betty will help with the typing.

你可以先寫草稿，然後貝蒂會幫忙打字。

複雜句 If it is possible, S + would like to + ...

如果可能的話，某人想……。

Ex If it is possible, I would like to work for the sales department.

如果有可能的話，我想在業務部工作。

7 購物篇

簡單句 Sth looks adj. ....

某物看起來……。

Ex That dress looks beautiful on you.

你穿那件洋裝真美。

複和句 V + O... or V + O....

……[做某事]，不然……。

Ex Buy it now or you'll be sorry.

趕快來買，不然你會後悔。

複雜句 When + S + V, S + V... at once....

當……，……馬上……。

Ex When the department store opens its door, Nick rushes into it at once.

當百貨公司開門時，尼克馬上衝進去。

8 公共服務篇

簡單句 fill in + N

填寫……。

Ex Fill in the form please.

請填一下這張表格。

複和句 Please V ..., and then....

請……，然後……。

Ex Please give me your ID card and then you can have the visitor's card.

先給我你的身分證，然後這張訪客證給你。

複雜句 S + V... after S + V....

……後，……。

Ex We need to send this package to the post office after we fill in the form.

我們完成表格填寫後，要把這件包裹送到郵局去。

9 情緒篇

簡單句 What's wrong with sb / sth?

……怎麼了？

Ex What's wrong with your cat?

你的貓怎麼了？

複和句 Let's V..., and V...!

讓我們……，然後……。

Ex Let's have a talk first, and see your parents later!

讓我們先好好聊聊，然後再去見你的父母。

複雜句 S + were / was + Ving...when S + V....

……的時候，某人（過去）（正在）……。

Ex David was jumping around like a monkey when I talked to his teacher.

我在跟老師講話的時候，大衛像隻猴子一樣的到處跳來跳去。

KNESS—A TIN

D FOR THE BEDSIDE LAMP AND TURNED IT

UINTING AT HIS SURROU

S, AND A COLOSSAL MAHOGANY FO

ILIAR RING. PR

ROOM WITH LOUIS XVI FURE, HAND-FRE S

SCOUR-POSTER BED.LA N

HONE WAS RINGING IN THE A

D FOR THE BEDSIDE LAMP AND TURNED IT

UINTING AT HIS SURROU

S, AND A COLOSSAL MAHOGANY FO

ROOM WITH LOUIS XVI FURE, HAND-FRE S

SCOUR-POSTER BED.LA N

IDE TABLE.TH

ON A CRUMPLED FLYER ON

OUDLY PRESENTSA

DON PROFESSOR O

Y. A VISITOR? HIS EYES FOC

BCAN UNIVERSITY OF

RIN EVENING

GIOUS SYMBOLOGY, HARV

NIVERSITY LANGDO

Chapter 1

Communication
交際篇

01 Meeting New Friends 認識新朋友

Dialogue 1 第一次聊就上手

track001

Jim: Lily, this is my friend, David.

Lily: Nice to meet you!

David: Nice to meet you, too.

Lily: How do you like China so far?

David: It's really not I expected before.

Lily: Don't worry. You'll get used to living here before long.

Translation 中譯照過來

吉姆：莉莉，這是我的朋友大衛。

莉莉：很高興見到你！

大衛：我也很高興見到你。

莉莉：到目前為止你覺得中國怎麼樣？

大衛：與我想像的很不一樣。

莉莉：別擔心。不久以後你就會適應這裡的生活了。

Key words 重點單字快速記

friend [frɛnd] 名. 朋友，友人
meet [mit] 動. 認識，結識；被引見（給某人）
expected [ɪk`spɛktɪd] 形. 預料中的
living [`lɪvɪŋ] 名. 生活
long [lɔŋ] 形. 長的

Patterns 延伸句型快速學

01 *How do you like + N ?*

（你覺得……怎麼樣？）

> How do you like my T-shirt?
> 你覺得我的 T 恤怎麼樣？

02 *S + get used to + Ving / N.*

（習慣於……；適應於……。）

> After Mary moved to London, she spent a lot of time getting used to the weather.
> 搬到倫敦以後，瑪莉花了很多時間適應天氣。

Common Sense 小常識

美國人怎樣稱呼對方

多數美國人喜歡別人直呼自己的名字，他們認為這樣顯得親切友好。當人們初次見面時，通常會連名帶姓一起介紹給對方，但雙方用不了多長時間就會直呼名字。當你剛剛結識一個美國人時，可以稱呼對方先生或女士，這時，對方通常會熱情地告訴你他的名字。

01 Meeting New Friends 認識新朋友

Dialogue 2 第一次聊就上手

track002

Kevin : Great party, isn't it?

Kate : Yeah. Lisa always has great parties.

Kevin : I only met Lisa last month. She and I work at the same hospital.

Kate : Oh, so you're a doctor?

Kevin : Yeah. How about you?

Kate : I'm a teacher.

Kevin : Oh, I see. By the way, my name's Kevin.

Kate : Nice to meet you. I'm Kate.

Translation 中譯照過來

凱文：很棒的聚會，是吧？

凱特：是呀。麗莎總是把聚會辦得很好。

凱文：我上個月才認識麗莎。她跟我在同一所醫院工作。

凱特：哦，這麼說你是個醫生了？

凱文：是的。你呢？

凱特：我是個老師。

凱文：原來如此。順便自我介紹一下，我叫凱文。

凱特：很高興認識你。我叫凱特。

Key words 重點單字快速記

always [ˋɔlwez] 副. 總是
hospital [ˋhɑspɪtḷ] 名. 醫院
doctor [ˋdɑktɚ] 名. 醫生
teacher [ˋtitʃɚ] 名. 老師
name [nem] 名. 名字

Patterns 延伸句型快速學

01 ***(It is a) NP, isn't it?***
（……，是吧？）

> It is a lovely house, isn't it?
> 這是一間可愛的房子，是吧？

02 ***By the way, ...***
（順帶一提，……。）

> I'm going to Jane's party. By the way, I am not going home tonight.
> 我正要去珍的派對。順帶一提，我今晚不會回家。

Common Sense 小常識

美國人怎樣稱呼對方

美國人之間不分年齡大小、職位高低，都以稱呼對方的名字來拉近彼此的距離。除法官、高級政府官員、軍官、醫生、教授和高級宗教人士外，美國人一般不會用正式頭銜稱呼別人。

Key Sentences 基本句大變身

track003

1 May I introduce myself? 我可以自我介紹一下嗎？

- Allow me to introduce myself, please. 請允許我自我介紹一下。
- Will you please introduce me to your friend?
  請你把我介紹給你的朋友好嗎？

2 My name is Judy. 我的名字叫茱蒂。

- I am Judy. 我是茱蒂。
- You can call me Judy. 你可以叫我茱蒂。

3 Who are you? 你是誰？

- May I have your name, please? 能告訴我你的名字嗎？
- What's your friend's name? 你的朋友叫什麼名字？

4 Let me introduce my friend Lily. 讓我來介紹一下我的朋友莉莉。

- I'd like you to meet my friend Lily.
  我想請你認識一下我的朋友莉莉。
- Meet my friend Lily, please. 請認識一下我的朋友莉莉。

5 How do you do? 你好。

- Nice to meet you. 很高興認識你。
- It's a pleasure to meet you. 很高興認識你。

6 I've heard so much about you. 我已經聽過關於你的好些事了。

- Jim has often talked about you. 吉姆老是提起你。

02 Old Friends Reunion 老友重逢

Dialogue 1 第一次聊就上手

track004

Jack : Helen? Hi!

Helen : Jack! Haven't seen you in ages! How have you been?

Jack : Good. I've been looking for a place to live these days.

Helen : Have you found yet?

Jack : No yet.

Helen : Well, maybe I can help. My friend Jim will go abroad. And if you are interested, you can go to have a look at his place.

Jack : Great. I know Jim. He is such a kind man.

Helen : OK. Then I will ask Jim when he's available to show the apartment and let you know.

Jack : Thank you.

Translation 中譯照過來

傑克：海倫？嗨！

海倫：傑克！好久沒見你了，最近怎麼樣？

傑克：很好。這些天我在找住的地方。

海倫：找到了嗎？

傑克：還沒呢。

海倫：好吧，也許我能幫到你。我的朋友吉姆要出國了，如果你有興趣的話可以去看看他的住處。

傑克：太棒了。我知道吉姆。他人超好的。

海倫：好的，那我會問問吉姆何時有空讓你看房子，然後告訴你。

傑克：謝謝。

Key words 重點單字快速記

maybe [ˋmebɪ] 副. 大概；或許
abroad [əˋbrɔd] 副. 海外
interested [ˋɪntərɪstɪd] 形. 感興趣的
kind [kaɪnd] 形. 親切的
available [əˋvelıbḷ] 形. （人）有空的；可用的，可獲得的

Patterns 延伸句型快速學

01 ***S + have / has not p.p. + O + in ages.***

（某人很久沒……。）

> Justin has not been out with a girl in ages.
> 賈斯汀很久沒跟女孩出去玩了。

02 ***If S + V, S ....***

（如果……。）

> If you want to finish the project on time, you can start it from now.
> 如果你想要準時完成這項計畫，你可以從現在就開始做。

Common Sense 小常識

與美國人交流的禁忌

●忌談錢

與美國人交談時不要把話題集中到錢上。談論別人的薪資和財產，被美國人認為是很沒素養的表現。

●忌談體重

在美國，談論體重是極其無禮的。體重屬於個人隱私，對此大發言論是不尊重他人的表現。

●忌談政治觀點

在美國，雖然談論政治觀點不是無法原諒的錯誤，但美國各種主流政治觀點較為寬鬆，談論話題應盡量避免政治字眼。

02 Old Friends Reunion 老友重逢

Dialogue 2 第一次聊就上手

track005

Lucy : How's it going?

Joey : I just find a job, so I'm busy learning everything.

Lucy : Have you finished school?

Joey : Yes, I joined the summer courses, so I finished school in advance.

Lucy : That's great. I'm really happy for you.

Joey : Thanks.

Translation 中譯照過來

露西：近來可好？

喬伊：我剛找到一份工作，所以在忙著學習所有的東西。

露西：你完成學業了嗎？

喬伊：是的。我參加了暑期課程，所以提前完成了學業。

露西：那太棒了，我真為你高興。

喬伊：謝謝。

Key words 重點單字快速記

job [dʒɑb] 名. 工作
busy [ˋbɪzɪ] 形. 忙碌的
learn [lɝn] 動. 學習
course [kors] 名. 課程
advance [ədˋvæns] 形. 預先的

Patterns 延伸句型快速學

01 *S + be + busy + Ving....*

（某人忙著做……。）

> The teacher is busy answering his students' questions.
> 那位老師正忙著回答學生們的問題。

02 *..., so ....*

（……，所以……。）

> It rained this morning, so the ground is wet now.
> 早上下過雨，所以現在地上是濕的。

Common Sense 小常識

與美國人交流的禁忌

●忌談宗教信仰

宗教信仰屬於個人隱私，平時交流中應盡量避免涉及該話題。

●忌談足球

這裡指的是 soccer（足球），而非 football（美式橄欖球）。足球在美國是相對冷門的運動，尤其是一些老頑固體育迷，對其有強烈的抵觸情緒，因此應盡量少提足球。

Key 基本句大變身 Sentences

track006

1 How's it going? 近來可好？

- How are you doing?
  最近怎麼樣？
- How have you been?
  最近怎麼樣？

2 You look great. 你看來氣色很好。

- You look pale. What's the matter with you?
  你臉色很蒼白，怎麼了？
- You look a bit worried.
  你看上去有點不開心。

3 Haven't seen you in ages. 很久沒見到你了。

- Haven't seen you for a long time.
  好久沒見到你了。
- I haven't seen you for so long.
  我好久沒見到你了。

4 What's new? 有什麼新鮮事嗎？

- What's new with you?
  你有什麼新鮮事嗎？

5 The same as usual. 和平時差不多。

- Nothing is special.
  沒什麼特別的。

03 Knowing the Neighbors 認識鄰居

Dialogue 1 第一次聊就上手

track007

Lucy : Did you just move here?
Peter : Yes, I moved in about two weeks ago.
Lucy : Do you have a lot of kids?
Peter : I have two children.
Lucy : How old are they?
Peter : My daughter is seven, while my son is five.
Lucy : Wow, that's great. I only have one child.
Peter : What's your child's age?
Lucy : She is only four years old.
Peter : So you have a daughter. She must be very cute.
Lucy : Thank you.

Translation 中譯照過來

露西：你剛剛搬到這兒嗎？
彼得：是的，我大概兩週前搬到這兒的。
露西：你有很多孩子嗎？
彼得：我有兩個孩子。
露西：他們多大了？
彼得：我女兒 7 歲了，我兒子 5 歲了。
露西：哇，太棒了。我只有一個孩子。
彼得：你的孩子多大了？
露西：她只有 4 歲。
彼得：所以你有一個女兒。她肯定非常可愛。
露西：謝謝。

Key words 重點單字快速記

neighbor [ˋnebɚ] 名. 鄰居；鄰國
move [muv] 動. 搬家，搬遷
child [tʃaɪld] 名. 孩子
daughter [ˋdɔtɚ] 名. 女兒
son [sʌn] 名. 兒子

Patterns 延伸句型快速學

01 ***S + V-ed (+ O) + 一段時間 + ago.***
（某人在～以前做了⋯⋯。）

> Tina witnessed the car accident two hours ago.
> 蒂娜在兩小時前目擊了那場車禍。

02 ***..., while ....***
（⋯⋯，而⋯⋯。）

> I like to go out, while my boyfriend likes to stay at home.
> 我喜歡外出，而我的男友喜歡待在家。

Common Sense 小常識

美國人與鄰居

美國初期人口稀少，因此美國人熱情好客，沒有築牆之城。美國人雖然普遍給人很獨立的印象，但他們多半不喜歡獨處，因此鄰居在美國人眼中是十分重要的。

03 Knowing the Neighbors 認識鄰居

Dialogue 2 第一次聊就上手

track008

Jim : Hello! Nice to meet you.

Kate : Nice to meet you, too.

Jim : When did you moved in?

Kate : Just this week.

Jim : I didn't even know the house sold out.

Kate : How many years have you been living in this block?

Jim : I've been living here for over 10 years.

Kate : Ten years? That is a very long time.

Jim : Yes, and I hope we can be neighbors for a while longer.

Kate : We will. I love this house very much.

Translation 中譯照過來

吉姆：你好！很高興見到你。

凱特：我也很高興見到你。

吉姆：你什麼時候搬進來的？

凱特：這週剛剛搬進來。

吉姆：我甚至都不知道這間房子賣出去了。

凱特：你在這個街區住了多少年了？

吉姆：我在這裡住了超過十年了。

凱特：十年？很長的時間啊。

吉姆：是的，我希望我們能夠長久的做鄰居。

凱特：我們會的。我非常喜歡這間房子。

Key words 重點單字快速記

know [no] 動. 熟悉，瞭解；知道
sell [sɛl] 動. 賣
block [blɑk] 名. 街區；塊
over [ˋovɚ] 介. 超過
house [haʊs] 名. 房子

Patterns 延伸句型快速學

01 *How many* + 可數名詞 ...?

（……有多少？）

How many days do you work in a week?
你一週工作多少天？

02 *S + have / has + been + Ving + for ....*

（某人仍持續做……。）

Sammy has been watching TV for three hours.
賽米看電視看了三個小時了。

Common Sense 小常識

美國人與鄰居

美國人的院子與鄰居的院子連在一起，有時不經過邀請，也不提前打個電話就會互相拜訪。部分美國家庭甚至會有玻璃牆或無門房間，可見他們渴望坦然相處的願望。

Key Sentences 基本句大變身

track009

1 It's a pleasure to meet you 很高興認識你。

- How nice to meet you.
  認識你真好。
- It's my pleasure to meet you.
  我很高興認識你。

2 I'm Mike, your new neighbor from this block. 我叫麥克，是你在這個街區的新鄰居。

- Hi! My name is Jack. I just moved in next door.
  你好！我叫傑克。我剛搬到隔壁。
- I'm John. We are neighborhood.
  我是約翰。我們是鄰居。

3 Where do you work? 你在哪裡工作？

- What do you do?
  你從事什麼工作？
- What's your job?
  你的工作是什麼？

4 Did you just move in this block? 你剛搬到這個街區嗎？

- How long have you lived here?
  你在這裡住多久了？
- Have you lived here for a long time?
  你在這裡住很久了嗎？

04 Inviting 邀請

Dialogue 1 第一次聊就上手

track010

Bob : Hi, Lisa.

Lisa : Hi, Bob.

Bob : Tomorrow's my birthday. I will hold a party at my house. Can you join us?

Lisa : When does the party start?

Bob : Seven o'clock in the evening. I'm inviting only a few friends. So please come.

Lisa : Of course, I'll come. Thank you for inviting me.

Bob : It's my pleasure.

Translation 中譯照過來

鮑勃：嗨，麗莎。

麗莎：嗨，鮑勃。

鮑勃：明天是我的生日。我會在自己的家裡舉辦一場聚會。你能加入我們嗎？

麗莎：聚會什麼時候開始？

鮑勃：晚上七點。我只邀請了幾個朋友。所以請你來吧。

麗莎：當然，我會去的。謝謝你邀請我。

鮑勃：這是我的榮幸。

Key words 重點單字快速記

birthday [ˋbɝθˏde] 名. 生日

hold [hold] 動. 舉辦

join [dʒɔɪn] 動. 參加

invite [ɪnˋvaɪt] 動. 邀請

pleasure [ˋplɛʒɚ] 名. 愉快；樂事

Patterns 延伸句型快速學

01 *S + will hold + NP....*

（某人將舉辦……。）

The professor in our department will hold an international meeting this week.

我們系上的教授本週將舉辦一場國際會議。

02 *Thank you for Ving + O.*

（謝謝你／你們……。）

Thank you for listening to my speech. Do you have any question?

謝謝你們聽我演說。你們有任何的問題嗎？

Common Sense 小常識

美國人的邀請

美國人邀請對方時通常會使用電話或當面邀請，作為受邀的人也要及時給予回復。若接受邀請後臨時有事不能前往，一定要及時通知邀請人。當天赴約時可以準時到達，也可推遲 5 到 10 分鐘趕到，給主人充裕的準備時間。

04 Inviting 邀請

Dialogue 2 第一次聊就上手

track011

David : Hello! Annie! How about going to the supermarket with me this afternoon?

Annie : I'd love to. But I've already had plans.

David : Then what about a rain check?

Annie : Yeah. How about tomorrow?

David : Good. So let's make it tomorrow morning, is that OK?

Annie : No problem. What about 9 o'clock?

David : Done. See you tomorrow.

Annie : See you.

Translation 中譯照過來

大衛：你好！安妮！今天下午和我一起去逛超市怎麼樣？

安妮：我很想去。但是我已經有其他安排了。

大衛：那另找時間怎麼樣？

安妮：好啊，明天怎麼樣？

大衛：好的，那麼我們約明天上午，可以嗎？

安妮：沒問題，9 點怎麼樣？

大衛：就這麼定了。明天見。

安妮：再見。

Key words 重點單字快速記

supermarket [ˋsupɚ͵mɑrkɪt] 名. 超市
afternoon [͵æftɚˋnun] 名. 下午
plan [plæn] 名. 計畫，打算
tomorrow [təˋmɔro] 名. 明天
done [dʌn] 形. 好

Patterns 延伸句型快速學

01 *How about + Ving + ... ?*

（……怎麼樣？）

> I don't know the answer, either. How about asking the teacher?
> 我也不知道答案。直接問老師怎麼樣？

02 *Let's + V + O.*

（習慣於……；適應於……。）

> We won first prize. Let's celebrate our winning!
> 我們拿下第一名。讓我們慶祝我們的獲勝！

Common Sense 小常識

美國人的邀請

若答應了美國人的邀約，卻必須遲到 15 分鐘以上，這時候別忘了給主人打電話告知緣由。用餐後也不要急著離開，可以閒聊大概半個小時，最後也要記得在離開前再次感謝主人的邀請。

Key 基本句大變身 Sentences

track012

1	Are you doing anything this after-noon?	你今天下午有安排嗎？

- Do you have plans for this afternoon?
  你今天下午有安排嗎？
- Are you busy this afternoon?
  今天下午你忙嗎？

2	What about having dinner togeth-er?	一起吃晚飯怎麼樣？

- How about having dinner together?
  一起吃晚飯怎麼樣？
- Let's have dinner together.
  我們一起吃晚飯吧。

3	Why don't we go to see a movie?	我們為什麼不去看電影呢？

- Why not go to see a movie?
  為什麼不去看電影呢？

4	How about the rain check?	另外找時間可以嗎？

- Can we plan it for another day?
  我們能約其他時間嗎？
- Let's do it another time.
  再找時間吧。

KNESS—A TIN
D FOR THE BEDSIDE LAMP AND TURNED IT
UINTING AT HIS SURROU
S, AND A COLOSSAL MAHOGANY FO
ILIAR RING. PI
ROOM WITH LOUIS XVI FURE, HAND-FRE S
SCOUR-POSTER BED.LA
HONE WAS RINGING IN THE A
D FOR THE BEDSIDE LAMP AND TURNED IT
UINTING AT HIS SURROU
S, AND A COLOSSAL MAHOGANY FO
ROOM WITH LOUIS XVI FURE, HAND-FRE S
SCOUR-POSTER BED.LA
IDE TABLE.TH
ON A CRUMPLED FLYER ON
OUDLY PRESENTSA
GDON PROFESSOR O
Y. A VISITOR? HIS EYES FOC
BCAN UNIVERSITY OF
RIN EVENING
GIOUS SYMBOLOGY, HARV
NIVERSITY LANGDO

Chapter 2

Transportation
交通運輸篇

05 Asking for Directions 問路

Dialogue 1 第一次聊就上手

track013

Helen: Excuse me? Can you show me where the Apple Avenue is?

Stranger : Of course. Go down this street and turn left at the first crossing. Then, you will see the Apple Avenue.

Helen : Great! Then I can find it easily. Is that far away from here?

Stranger : No. It's only ten minutes' walk.

Helen : That's good. Thanks.

Stranger : You're welcome.

Translation 中譯照過來

海倫：不好意思，您能告訴我蘋果大街在哪裡嗎？

路人：當然。沿著這條路一直走，在第一個十字路口左轉。然後你就可以看見蘋果大街了。

海倫：太好了！那我很容易就能找到了。它離這裡遠嗎？

路人：不遠。走路只要十分鐘。

海倫：太好了。謝謝。

路人：不用謝。

Key words 重點單字快速記

show [ʃo] 動. 指示
avenue [ˋævə͵nju] 名. 大街
street [strit] 名. 街
easily [ˋizɪlɪ] 副. 輕易地
walk [wɔk] 動. 走路

Patterns 延伸句型快速學

01 *Can you show me ...?*

（你可以告訴我……嗎？）

Can you show me how to solve this math question?
你可以告訴我怎麼解這題數學題嗎？

02 *A be far away from B.*

（A 地距離 B 地遙遠。）

The supermarket is far away from our home, so we need to go there by car.
超級市場距離我們家很遠，所以我們需要開車去那裡。

Common Sense 小常識

在美國問路

在美國問路是一件非常困難的事情，因為路上可以供你詢問的人少之又少，如果真的遇見什麼人，那你可以算得上是幸運兒了。美國人對問路的人通常都會十分熱情，也十分有耐心，有時甚至會為你畫張「地圖」來指路，如果條件允許的話，他們甚至願意直接帶你去目的地。

Key Sentences 基本句大變身

track014

1 Where am I? 我在哪裡？

- Can you tell me where I am?
  你能告訴我我在哪裡嗎？
- Could you please point out where I am on the map?
  你能在地圖上指出我在什麼地方嗎？

2 Where is the nearest post office? 最近的郵局在哪裡？

- Could you tell me the way to the nearest post office?
  你能告訴我最近的郵局怎麼走嗎？
- Do you know where the nearest post office is?
  你知道最近的郵局在哪裡嗎？

3 The nearest way is to go down to Apple Avenue and turn right. 最近的路線就是直走到蘋果大街再向右轉。

- The easiest way is to take Highway 3.
  最簡單的路是走三號高速公路。
- Go down this street for about 500 meters and turn left.
  沿著這條街走大約 500 公尺然後向左轉。

4 How far is it from here? 它距離這裡有多遠？

- How far away is it?
  有多遠？
- Is it far away from here?
  距離這裡遠嗎？

06 Driving 開車出遊

Dialogue 1 第一次聊就上手

track015

Clerk : What can I do for you?
Judy : I want to rent a car.
Clerk : What size do you prefer?
Judy : I'll take a small car. How much is it?
Clerk : Fifteen dollars a day. How long would you like to rent?
Judy : Six days.
Clerk : Can I have your name and address?
Judy : My name is Judy Green. I am from New York.
Clerk : Please show me your driver's license and a credit card.
Judy : Here you are.
Clerk : Great. Can I charge it on this card?
Judy : Yes. That's OK.

Translation 中譯照過來

接待員：我可以為您做點什麼嗎？
朱　迪：我想租輛車。
接待員：您想找什麼規格的車？
朱　迪：我想租一輛小型汽車。租金是多少呢？
接待員：一天 15 美元。您要租多久？
朱　迪：6 天。
接待員：能告訴我您的名字和地址嗎？
朱　迪：我叫朱迪 · 格林，來自紐約。
接待員：請讓我看一下您的駕照和信用卡。
朱　迪：給你。
接待員：好的。我可以用這張信用卡收費嗎？
朱　迪：好的。用那張就行。

Key words 重點單字快速記

rent [rɛnt] 動.（短期）租用
size [saɪz] 名. 規格、尺寸
address [ə ˋdrɛs] 名. 地址
license [ˋlaɪsn̩s] 名. 許可證，執照
credit card [ˋkrɛdɪt kɑrd] 名. 信用卡

Patterns 延伸句型快速學

01 ***How much* + 不可數名詞 + *aux. / be + S + V ?***
（……多少？）

How much exercise do you take every week?
你每週運動（量）多少？

02 ***How long + aux. / be + S + V ?***
（……多久？）

How long did the meeting last?
這場會議持續多久？

Common Sense 小常識

在美國幫汽車加油（1）

美國的加油站基本都是自助加油，無人服務。那麼我們該如何加油呢？

1. 刷信用卡加油：大部分加油機可以刷信用卡，具體操作步驟按照加油機提示即可，大體為：刷卡——選卡型——選油品——取加油槍加油——將加油槍放回——列印收據。

待續……

06 Driving 開車出遊

Dialogue 2 第一次聊就上手

track016

Clerk : Can I help you?

Peter : I'd like to rent a midsize car. How much is it?

Clerk : It's 25 dollars a day.

Peter : I need to rent the car for six days.

Clerk : Would you like to cover insurance?

Peter : How much is it?

Clerk : It's six dollars a day. It covers everything regardless of anyone's fault.

Peter : OK.

Translation 中譯照過來

職員：我能幫您做什麼嗎？

彼得：我想要租一輛中型車，請問多少錢？

職員：每一天是 25 美元。

彼得：我要租 6 天。

職員：您要為車辦理保險嗎？

彼得：多少錢？

職員：每天 6 美元。它涵蓋了一切故障和事故，不管是誰的過錯。

彼得：好的。

Key words 重點單字快速記

cover [ˋkʌvɚ] 動. 為……保險
insurance [ɪnˋʃurəns] 名. 保險
everything [ˋɛvrɪˏθɪŋ] 代. 一切事物
regardless [rɪˋgardlɪs] 形. 不關心的
fault [fɔlt] 名. 過失

Patterns 延伸句型快速學

01 ***I'd like to V ....***
（我想要……。）

I'd like to have a drink.
我想要一杯飲料。

02 ***S + V + O + regardless of + N.***
（不管／不顧……。）

The man decided to go outside regardless of the heavy rain.
那男人決定外出，不管外頭的大雨。

Common Sense 小常識

在美國幫汽車加油（2）

前面講過，美國的加油站多半是自助加油，到底怎樣才能順利加油呢？接著看吧！

2. 自行加油後到收費處繳費：有很多加油機是可以先加油後繳費的，加好油後去收費處繳費，但美國無人監督。值得注意的是，如果沒有付錢就離開，被警察抓住的話，可是一生都不能再駕車了呢！

3. 用加油卡加油：部分加油站要求先到收費處繳費，拿到一次性加油卡後才可以加油。

Key Sentences 基本句大變身

track017

1 I need to rent a car. 我需要租輛車。

- Do you have any cars available?
  你們有車可以出租嗎？
- I'll take a midsize car.
  我想租一輛中型車。

2 Is it all right to park here? 可以在這裡停車嗎？

- Is it allowed to park there?
  可以在那裡停車嗎？
- Can I park here?
  我能在這裡停車嗎？

3 The car is out of gas. 車沒油了。

- My car runs out of gas.
  我的車沒有油了。
- The gas tank is empty.
  油箱空了。

4 My car can't start. 我的車發動不起來了。

- My car broke down.
  我的車拋錨了。
- My tire blew out.
  我的車爆胎了。

07 By Bike 騎腳踏車

Dialogue 1 第一次聊就上手

track018

Bob : Caroline, do you know any place where I can rent a bike?

Caroline : I don't know. Why not buy one?

Bob : Good idea. What kind of bike do you think suits me better?

Caroline : I think you can buy a mountain bike.

Bob : OK. I will get one as soon as possible. And then we can travel by bike.

Caroline : Yeah. It is more convenient than travel by bus.

Bob : That's true. We can see the scenery along the way. And riding a bike can make us healthier.

Caroline : Yeah. I agree with you.

Translation 中譯照過來

鮑　勃：卡洛琳，你知道哪裡有出租腳踏車嗎？

卡洛琳：我不知道。你為什麼不買一輛呢？

鮑　勃：好主意。你認為什麼樣的腳踏車更適合我？

卡洛琳：我覺得你可以買輛登山用腳踏車。

鮑　勃：好的，我盡快買一輛。這樣我們就能騎腳踏車出遊了。

卡洛琳：是啊。那比坐公車方便多了

鮑　勃：沒錯。我們可以欣賞沿途的風景，而且騎腳踏車可以讓我們更健康。

卡洛琳：是的，我同意你的觀點。

Key words 重點單字快速記

bike [baɪk] 名. 腳踏車
mountain [ˋmaʊntn̩] 名. 山
travel [ˋtrævl̩] 動. 旅遊
convenient [kənˋvinjənt] 形. 方便的，便利的
scenery [ˋsinərɪ] 名. 風景，自然景色

Patterns 延伸句型快速學

01 *... as soon as possible.*
（盡快……。）

> If you have any question, please mail me as soon as possible.

如果你有任何問題，請盡快寄信給我。

02 *A be more adj. than B.*
（A 比 B 更……。）

> In Tim's opinion, family is more important than career life.
> 依提姆之見，家庭比事業更重要。

Common Sense 小常識

在美國騎腳踏車

腳踏車在美國大多作為健身工具使用，被當作交通工具的情況極為少見。但有些住在大學校內或離學校較近的學生也會把腳踏車當作交通工具。需要注意的是，美國大多數學校都要求騎腳踏車的學生向校內警察登記，以此來防止車輛被盜，如果違規不登記的話，還有可能會被罰款。此外，在美國騎腳踏車是比較危險的，一定要注意個人安全。

Key Sentences 基本句大變身

track019

1 I want to buy a bike. 我想買一輛腳踏車。

- I'd like to buy a mountain bike.
  我想買一輛登山用腳踏車。
- I want to buy a fixed gear bike.
  我想買一輛單速腳踏車。

2 Can I give it a shot? 我能試騎一下嗎？

- Can I give it a try?
  我能試騎一下嗎？
- Can I give it a go?
  我能試騎一下嗎？

3 Biking is good for health. 騎車對身體好。

- Biking makes us healthier.
  騎腳踏車讓我們更健康。
- Biking is a good exercise.
  騎腳踏車是一項很好的體育鍛鍊。

4 The chain of the bike comes off. 腳踏車鍊子掉了。

- My bike was broken down.
  我的腳踏車壞了。
- There is something wrong with my bike.
  我的腳踏車出了問題。

08 By Taxi 搭乘計程車

Dialogue 1 第一次聊就上手

track020

Julie : Taxi!

Taxi driver : Where would you like to go?

Julie : I would like to go to the train stop. Can we get there before 4 o'clock?

Taxi driver : Yes, we can get there on time if there is no traffic jam.

Julie : Can we stop at the bank? I want to withdraw some money.

Taxi driver : OK. I'll wait for you here.

(after a while)

Julie : Thanks. We can go now.

Taxi driver : OK.

(later)

Taxi driver : Here we are. That's 20 dollars.

Julie : Here you are. Keep the change.

Taxi driver : Thank you.

Translation 中譯照過來

朱莉：計程車！

計程車司機：您要去哪裡？

朱莉：我要去火車站。我們在 4 點之前能趕到嗎？

計程車司機：是的。如果交通不堵塞，我們可以趕到。

朱莉：我們能在那家銀行停一下嗎？我想領一些錢。

計程車司機：好的，我在這裡等你。

（過了一會兒）

朱莉：謝謝。我們現在可以走了。

計程車司機：好的。

（稍後）

計程車司機：我們到了。總共是 20 美元。

朱莉：給你錢，不用找了。

計程車司機：謝謝。

Key words 重點單字快速記

taxi [ˋtæksɪ] 名. 計程車
train [tren] 名. 火車
traffic [ˋtræfɪk] 名. 交通
bank [bæŋk] 名. 銀行
change [tʃendʒ] 名. 找回的零錢

Patterns 延伸句型快速學

01 *There is no ....*

（沒有任何……。）

> The boss says there is no reason to delay the project, and he asks us to turn in the report on time.
>
> 老闆說沒有任何理由延誤計畫，他要求我們準時繳交報告。

02 *Here you are.*

（這給你。／拿去吧。）

> A : May I borrow your scissors? B : Here you are.
>
> A：我可以借你的剪刀嗎？B：（剪刀）拿去吧。

Common Sense 小常識

美國的計程車

在美國的城市中心和機場附近，計程車隨處可見，招手即來。但在其他大部分地區想要搭計程車時，就需要打電話叫車。美國計程車大多數根據路程計費，計價表通常會貼在車內。

08 By Taxi 搭乘計程車

Dialogue 2 第一次聊就上手

track021

John : Taxi! Can you take me to the Central Park?

Taxi driver : Yes. It's my pleasure to serve you.

John : Can you help me to put the baggage in the trunk?

Taxi driver : Certainly.

John : Can you open the window? I feel too close.

Taxi driver : OK. Sorry, I'm afraid we can't pass the street because of the traffic jam.

John : Shall we take the shortcut?

Taxi driver : OK, I will find another way.

Translation 中譯照過來

約　　翰：計程車！你能把我帶到中央公園嗎？

計程車司機：好的。很高興為您服務。

約　　翰：你能幫我把行李放到後車箱嗎？

計程車司機：當然。

約　　翰：你能打開窗戶嗎？我感覺很悶。

計程車司機：好的。抱歉，因為交通堵塞，恐怕我們不能通過這條街了。

約　　翰：我們可以走捷徑嗎？

計程車司機：好的，我會找到另一條路的。

Key words 重點單字快速記

serve [sɝv] 動. 為（顧客）服務
baggage [ˋbægɪdʒ] 名. 行李
trunk [trʌŋk] 名. 汽車的後行李箱
close [kloz] 形. 悶熱的
shortcut [ˋʃɔrtˏkʌt] 名. 近路；捷徑

Patterns 延伸句型快速學

01 *Can you help me (to) V + O ?*

（你能幫我……嗎？）

Can you help me to mop the floor?
你能幫我拖地嗎？

02 *S + V + O + because of + N.*

（因為……，所以……。）

The train delayed 40 minutes because of the car accident.
因為車禍，那台火車延誤了 40 分鐘。

Common Sense 小常識

美國的計程車

在美國乘坐計程車，到達目的地後，記得給計程車司機車資百分之十到百分之二十的小費，有時也可以根據行李件數計算小費，通常以一件行李一美元計算。

Key Sentences 基本句大變身

track022

1 I'd like to go to the airport. 我要去機場。

- Could you take me to the railway station?
  你能帶我去火車站嗎？
- I want to go to this address, please.
  拜託，我要去這裡。

2 Can you help me to put the luggage in the trunk? 你能幫我把行李放到後車箱嗎？

- Please put my baggage in the back.
  請把我的行李放到後面。

3 Can you speed up a bit more? 再快一點可以嗎？

- Please slow down.
  請開慢一點。
- Can you take the shortest way, please?
  你能走最短的路線嗎？

4 Here is the money. 給你錢。

- Here is the tip.
  這是小費。
- Keep the change.
  零錢不用找了。

09 By Bus 搭乘公車

Dialogue 1 第一次聊就上手

track023

Kate : Jim, how do we go to the park?
Jim : We can go there by bus.
Kate : Which bus should we take?
Jim : We can take No. 6 bus.
Kate : Are you sure?
Jim : Yes. I always catch this bus.
Kate : How long does it take?
Jim : It takes only an hour.
Kate : Which stop should we get off at?
Jim : We can get off at the Apple Avenue Stop.
Kate : That's great.

Translation 中譯照過來

凱特：吉姆，我們怎麼去公園？
吉姆：我們可以坐公車去。
凱特：我們應該乘坐哪路公車？
吉姆：我們可以乘坐 6 路公車。
凱特：你確定嗎？
吉姆：是的，我一直都坐這班車。
凱特：大概需要多長時間？
吉姆：只需要一個小時。
凱特：我們在哪站下車？
吉姆：我們應該在蘋果大街站下車。
凱特：太棒了。

Key words 重點單字快速記

by [baɪ] 介. 透過
bus [bʌs] 名. 公車
park [pɑrk] 名. 公園
take [tek] 動. 乘坐；花費；做
stop [stɑp] 名. 車站

Patterns 延伸句型快速學

01 *Which N + be / aux. + S (+ V)?*
（……哪一個？）

There are Team Red, Team Yellow, and Team Blue.
Which team do you want to join?
這裡有紅隊、黃隊和藍隊。你想加入哪一隊？

02 *Sth takes / took (+ O) ....*
（某事花費了……。）

Doing the homework took me three hours.
做回家功課花了我 3 個小時。

Common Sense 小常識

美國的公車

美國大部分城市都有公車，公車路線四通八達。跟台灣相同，美國的公車票價也較為低廉，一美元到數美元不等。美國的公車站牌上也都有公車行駛路線和時刻表。

09 By Bus 搭乘公車

Dialogue 2 第一次聊就上手

track024

Jerry : Do you know when the bus will come here?
Lisa : Which bus?
Jerry : The No. 5 bus.
Lisa : It will come here in five minutes.
Jerry : Thank you. I'm Jerry. Nice to meet you.
Lisa : I'm Lisa. I will take the same bus.
Jerry : Does the bus go to the Central Park?
Lisa : Yes.
Jerry : How long will it take to get there?
Lisa : About two hours.
Jerry : Wow, what a long trip!

Translation 中譯照過來

傑瑞：你知道公車什麼時候來嗎？
麗莎：哪一路公車？
傑瑞：5 路公車。
麗莎：五分鐘後就會來。
傑瑞：謝謝。我叫傑瑞，很高興認識你。
麗莎：我叫麗莎。我也乘坐同一路公車。
傑瑞：這路公車開往中央公園嗎？
麗莎：是的。
傑瑞：要多久才能到達那裡？
麗莎：大概兩個小時。
傑瑞：哇，好長的一段旅程啊！

Key words 重點單字快速記

which [hwɪtʃ] 代. 哪一個
minute [ˋmɪnɪt] 名. 分鐘
same [sem] 形. 同樣的
long [lɔŋ] 形. 長的
trip [trɪp] 名. 旅行，出行

Patterns 延伸句型快速學

01 *Do you know when ...?*
（你知道某物什麼時候……？）

Do you know when the typhoon will come?
你知道颱風什麼時候來嗎？

02 *What + a / an + adj. + N!*
（好……的某物！）

What a lovely couple!
好可愛的一對情侶啊！

Common Sense 小常識

美國的公車

跟台灣不同的是，美國公車上乘坐的人一般較少，不會像台灣一樣出現人潮擁擠的現象，而且美國公車兩趟車之間間隔的時間也相對較長。

Key Sentences 基本句大變身

track025

1 Does this bus go to the zoo? 這班公車開往動物園嗎？

- I want to know if this is the right bus to the zoo.
  我想知道這是否是去動物園的公車。

2 Does anyone sit here? 這裡有人坐嗎？

- Can I sit here?
  我可以坐這裡嗎？
- Is this seat taken?
  這個座位有人坐嗎？

3 What stop are we at? 我們到哪一站了？

- What's the next stop?
  下一站是哪兒？
- Which stop do we get off at?
  我們在哪一站下車？

4 I think we got on the wrong bus. 我想我們坐錯車了。

- Are you sure that we got on the right bus?
  你確定我們坐對車了嗎？
- Is this the right bus, or not?
  我們有沒有坐對車？

10 By Train 搭乘火車

Dialogue 1 第一次聊就上手

track026

Jack : I need a ticket to Washington.

Ticket agent : What do you want, a one-way or a round-trip ticket?

Jack : Round-trip, please.

Ticket agent : Please show me your passport and ID card.

Jack : Here you are.

Ticket agent : OK. The fare is 40 dollars.

Jack : Well. How long will it take to reach Washington?

Ticket agent : About two hours.

Jack : OK. Thank you.

Translation 中譯照過來

傑　克：我需要一張到華盛頓的火車票。

售票員：您想要單程票還是往返票？

傑　克：往返票。

售票員：請出示您的護照和身分證件。

傑　克：給你。

售票員：好的，票價是 40 美元。

傑　克：好吧。到達華盛頓要多長時間？

售票員：大約兩個小時。

傑　克：好的。謝謝。

Key words 重點單字快速記

agent [ˋedʒənt] 名. 代理人
way [we] 名. 方向
round [raʊnd] 副. 循環地
passport [ˋpæs͵port] 名. 護照
card [kɑrd] 名. 卡片
fare [fɛr] 名. 票價

Patterns 延伸句型快速學

01 *What do you want, A or B ?*

（你想要什麼，A或是B？）

What do you want, to stay at home or to go out and have fun?
你想要什麼，待在家裡還是出去找點樂子？

02 *N, please.*

（請給我……。）

A : What would you like to drink? B : Coke, please.
A：你想喝點什麼？B：請給我可樂。

Common Sense 小常識

美國火車

美國火車公司以美國國家鐵路客運公司（National Railroad Passenger Corporation of the USA，常用商標為Amtrak）為主，乘坐該公司的火車既舒適又可觀光。座位空間寬敞又乾淨。

10 By Train 搭乘火車

Dialogue 2 第一次聊就上手

track027

Kevin : Excuse me. When does the No. 6 train leave?
Ticket agent : At 15:30.
Kevin : Is it a direct train?
Ticket agent : Yes, it is.
Kevin : OK. Three tickets for No. 6 train, please.
Ticket agent : One-way or round-trip?
Kevin : Round-trip, please. How much in total?
Ticket agent : 60 dollars.
Kevin : Here you are. Can you tell me which platform should I go to wait for the train?
Ticket agent : It's platform 9.
Kevin : OK. Thank you.
Ticket agent : You are welcome.

Translation 中譯照過來

凱　文：請問一下，6 號車幾點出發？
票務員：15:30 出發。
凱　文：是直達的嗎？
票務員：是的，是直達的。
凱　文：好的，請給我三張 6 號車車票。
票務員：單程的還是往返的？
凱　文：往返的。一共多少錢？
票務員：60 美元。
凱　文：給你錢。你能告訴我我該去哪個月臺等車嗎？
票務員：9 號月臺。
凱　文：好的，謝謝。
票務員：不客氣。

Key words 重點單字快速記

leave [liv] 動. 離開
direct [dəˋrɛkt] 形. 直達的
ticket [ˋtɪkɪt] 名. 票
total [ˋtotl̩] 名. 總數
platform [ˋplæt͵fɔrm] 名. 月臺

Patterns 延伸句型快速學

01 *Excuse me.*
（不好意思。）

> Excuse me. Is this seat available?
> 不好意思，這個座位是空的嗎？

02 *Can you tell me ...?*
（你能告訴我……嗎？）

> Can you tell me where Tammy is?
> 你能告訴我泰咪在哪裡嗎？

Common Sense 小常識

美國火車

在美國，長線的火車通常分為兩層，一層是廁所和放行李的地方，二層是座位。最吸引人的地方是火車上還設有更衣室，裡面備有小沙發，供乘客更換衣服使用。

Key 基本句大變身 Sentences

track028

1 Is there any express train to Washington? 有到華盛頓的特快列車嗎？

- Is there any fast train to Washington?
  有到華盛頓的快速列車嗎？
- Is there a through train to Washington?
  有到華盛頓的直達列車嗎？

2 When does No.5 train leave? 5 號車什麼時候出發？

- At what time does No.5 train leave?
  5 號車什麼時候出發？
- When does No.5 train arrive?
  5 號車什麼時候到達？

3 How much is the fare? 票價是多少？

- How much is a ticket to New York?
  到紐約一張票多少錢？
- I want to buy a ticket to New York.
  我想買一張到紐約的票。

4 Which platform is for No. 3 train? 3 號列車在哪個月臺？

- Where is the No. 2 platform?
  2 號月臺在哪裡？
- Which platform does the No.5 train leave from?
  5 號列車從哪個月臺出發？

11 By Subway 搭乘地鐵

Dialogue 1 第一次聊就上手

track029

Kate : How can we get to the Central Park, please?

Ticket agent : You can take Line 3.

Kate : Then how much is it?

Ticket agent : 2.75 dollars.

Kate : Which way should I go for Line 3?

Ticket agent : Just follow the signs.

Kate : I see. Thank you.

Translation 中譯照過來

凱　特：請問去中央公園怎麼走？

票務員：你可以坐 3 號線。

凱　特：票價多少？

票務員：2.75 美元。

凱　特：我應該怎麼去 3 號線？

票務員：跟著指示牌走就可以了。

凱　特：我明白了。謝謝你。

Key words 重點單字快速記

central [ˋsɛntrəl] 形. 中央的
subway [ˋsʌbˏwe] 名. 地鐵
line [laɪn] 名. 路線
follow [ˋfɑlo] 動. 跟隨
sign [saɪn] 名. 指示牌，標示牌

Patterns 延伸句型快速學

01 *Which way + aux. + S + V?*
（某人怎麼去……？）

> Which way should I go to the train station?
> 我應該怎麼去火車站？

02 *I see.*
（我明白了。）

> A: Do not use your camera in the museum.
> B: I see.
> A：不要在博物館內使用相機。B：我明白了。

Common Sense 小常識

美國的地鐵

在美國，只有東部城市才有地鐵。那麼該怎樣搭乘地鐵呢？以紐約為例，紐約地鐵通常需要購買地鐵（MTA）卡，該卡在任何地鐵站自動售票機上均可購買或加值。

11 By Subway 搭乘地鐵

Dialogue 2 第一次聊就上手

track030

Jim : Where can I buy a ticket?

Ticket agent : You need to go to the ticket office.

Jim : So I can use the ticket to enter?

Ticket agent : Yes. You can press the ticket at the entrance, and the door will be open automatically.

Jim : OK, I know. Thank you very much.

Translation 中譯照過來

吉　姆：我可以在哪裡買票？

票務員：你需要去售票處。

吉　姆：所以我可以用地鐵票進站嗎？

票務員：是的，你可以把票放在入口處，門就會自動打開。

吉　姆：好的，我知道了。非常感謝。

Key words 重點單字快速記

enter [ˋɛntɚ] 動. 進入
press [prɛs] 動. 按，壓
entrance [ˋɛntrəns] 名. （場所的）門，入口，通道
open [ˋopən] 動. 打開
automatically [ˏɔtəˋmætɪklɪ] 副. （機器）自動地

Patterns 延伸句型快速學

01 ***S + need / needs / needed to + ...***
（某人必須要……。）

To earn more money, Vincent needs to take two jobs at the same time.
為了賺更多的錢，文森必須要同時做兩份工作。

02 ***..., and ....***
（……，……就會……。）

Enter your password, and the system will verify your identity automatically.
輸入你的密碼，系統就會自動驗證你的身分。

Common Sense 小常識

美國的地鐵

在美國乘坐地鐵，單次票價 2.75 美元。此外還有週票和月票，價格分別為 31 美元和 116.5 美元。乘坐一次地鐵即可免費乘坐一次公車。但紐澤西地鐵（包括公車）和紐約地鐵（也包括公車）之間是不能用一票換乘的。

Key Sentences 基本句大變身

track031

1	Which line goes to the library?	去圖書館應該坐哪條線？

- Which line should I take to the library?
  我應該乘坐哪條線去圖書館？
- Which line do I take for the library?
  去圖書館乘坐哪條線？

2	You can change to Line 3 at this station.	你可以在這一站換乘 3 號線。

- Which stop can I change to Line 3?
  到哪個站可以換乘地鐵 3 號線？
- I need to change to another line.
  我需要換乘另一條路線的車。

3	You can get off at this station.	你可以在這一站下車。

- Which stop shall I get off at?
  我應該在哪站下車？
- Get off at the third stop and then change to Line 3.
  在第三站下車，然後換乘 3 號線。

4	How often does the subway come?	地鐵多久會來一班？

- How frequent is the subway service?
  地鐵多久會來一班？

12 By Airplane 搭飛機

Dialogue 1 第一次聊就上手

track032

Check-in Operator : Good Morning.

Jack : Good Morning. Is this the right desk? My flight is AB123.

Check-in Operator : Yes, that's right. Please show me your passport and ticket.

Jack : Here you are.

Check-in Operator : Thank you. Do you have any baggage to check?

Jack : Yes, I have three suitcases.

Check-in Operator : You need to put them on the conveyor belt.

Jack : OK.

Check-in Operator : Do you like a window seat or an aisle seat?

Jack : A window seat, please.

Check-in Operator : OK. Here are your baggage tags and your boarding card. Your seat is 38BA.

Jack : Thank you.

Translation 中譯照過來

地勤人員：早安。

傑　　克：早安。是在這個櫃臺嗎？我的航班是 AB123。

地勤人員：是的，就是這裡。請讓我看一下您的護照和機票。

傑　　克：給你。

地勤人員：謝謝。您有要托運的行李嗎？

傑　　克：是的，我有三個手提箱。

地勤人員：您需要把它們放到傳送帶上。

傑　　克：好的。

地勤人員：您想要靠窗的座位還是靠走道的座位？

傑　　克：靠窗的座位。

地勤人員：好的。這是您的行李條和登機卡。您的座位是 38BA。

傑　　克：謝謝。

Key words 重點單字快速記

baggage [ˋbægɪdʒ] 名 行李
suitcase [ˋsut͵kes] 名（旅行用的）手提箱
belt [bɛlt] 名 長條帶狀物
aisle [aɪl] 名 通道，過道
seat [sit] 名 座位
tag [tæg] 名 標籤，標牌

Patterns 延伸句型快速學

01 *Please show me + N ....*

（請給我看……。）

Please show me your license and registration.
請給我看你的駕照和行照。

02 *Do you like A or B?*

（你想要A或B？）

Do you like coffee or tea?
你想要咖啡或茶？

Common Sense 小常識

購買飛機票

乘坐飛機前首先要購買機票，那麼什麼時候購買機票最為適宜呢？

在美國，購買機票一定要提前做好計畫，越早買越好。通常情況下，在出發日期的兩個星期前購票會相對便宜一點。

12 By Airplane 搭飛機

Dialogue 2 第一次聊就上手

track033

Ticket agent : What can I do for you?

Elena : I want to make a plane reservation to New York.

Ticket agent : May I have your name, please?

Elena : Elena Gilbert. I want to leave on March 31st.

Ticket agent : OK. What kind of ticket do you like?

Elena : I need an economy ticket.

Ticket agent : One-way or round-trip?

Elena : Round-trip, please. How much?

Ticket agent : Five hundred dollars.

Elena : OK. Here you are.

Ticket agent : Thank you.

Translation 中譯照過來

票務員：我能為您做點什麼嗎？

埃琳娜：我想預訂到紐約的機票。

票務員：能告訴我您的姓名嗎？

埃琳娜：埃琳娜 · 吉伯特。我想在 3 月 31 號出發。

票務員：好的，您想要什麼種類的機票？

埃琳娜：我要一張經濟艙的票。

票務員：單程的還是往返的？

埃琳娜：往返的。多少錢？

票務員：500 美元。

埃琳娜：好的，給你錢。

票務員：謝謝。

Chapter1 交際篇
Chapter2 交通運輸篇
Chapter3 用餐事宜篇
Chapter4 愛情篇
Chapter5 校園生活篇
Chapter6 工作篇
Chapter7 購物篇
Chapter8 公共服務篇
Chapter9 情緒篇

Key words 重點單字快速記

plane [plen] 名. 飛機
reservation [ˌrɛzɚˋveʃən] 名. （房間、座位等的）預訂
kind [kaɪnd] 名. 種類
economy [ɪˋkɑnəmɪ] 形. 經濟的
hundred [ˋhʌndrəd] 名. （一）百

Patterns 延伸句型快速學

01 *May I ...?*
（我能……嗎？）

May I have a moment, please?
我能擁有一分鐘嗎？（＝能給我一分鐘嗎？）

02 *What kind of + N + do you like?*
（你想要什麼種類的……？）

What kind of movie do you like, scary or romance?
你想要什麼種類的電影，恐怖片還是愛情片？

Common Sense 小常識

購買飛機票

在美國，如果在出發日前一個星期前購買票價會加倍，一個星期之內購買，票價會再翻一倍。需要注意的是，美國航空公司時常會推出減價機票，而且減幅很大，旅客一定要抓住這樣的好時機。

Key Sentences 基本句大變身

track034

1 I'd like to book a ticket for May 31st. 我想訂一張 5 月 31 日的票

- I want to book a flight to New York.
  我要訂一張去紐約的機票。
- I'd like a one-way ticket to Beijing.
  我要一張去北京的單程票。
- I want to make a plane reservation to New York.
  我想預訂到紐約的機票。

2 What's the departure time? 什麼時候起飛？

- What time does it take off?
  什麼時候起飛？
- What's the arrival time?
  何時抵達？

3 Can I change my flight schedule? 我可以更改航班嗎？

- I need to reschedule my flight.
  我要更改航班。
- I would like to cancel my flight.
  我想要取消航班。

4 Could I exchange seats with you? 我能和你換個位子嗎？

- Would you mind exchanging seats with me?
  你介意和我換下位子嗎？
- I am wondering if you can exchange seat with me.
  我在想你是否願意和我換一下座位。

13 Traffic Block 交通堵塞

Dialogue 1 第一次聊就上手

track035

Gill : Excuse me. Can you tell me why the traffic is so heavy?

Stranger : Two cars crashed into each other and blocked the road.

Gill : Oh my God. Did anyone hurt?

Stranger : Luckily, nobody was hurt.

Gill : That's good. But now we have to wait.

Stranger : Don't worry. It's said that the traffic jam will be over soon.

Gill : Really? Oh, that's great.

Translation 中譯照過來

吉爾：打擾一下。你能告訴我為什麼交通這麼堵塞嗎？

路人：有兩輛小汽車相撞，堵住了道路。

吉爾：噢，天哪！有人受傷了嗎？

路人：很幸運，沒有人受傷。

吉爾：那就好。但是我們現在只能等著。

路人：別擔心，我聽說交通擁擠的情況很快就會結束了。

吉爾：真的嗎？噢，太好了。

Key words 重點單字快速記

traffic [ˋtræfɪk] 名. 交通

heavy [ˋhɛvɪ] 形. 大量的，很多的

block [blɑk] 名. 障礙，阻礙　動. 阻擋，阻塞

road [rod] 名. 道路

crash [kræʃ] 動. 撞車

Patterns 延伸句型快速學

01 *Can you tell me why ...?*

（你能告訴我為什麼……嗎？）

> Can you tell me why you won't attend my birthday party?
>
> 你能告訴我為什麼你不能出席我的生日派對嗎？

02 *It is / was said that ....*

（聽說……。）

> It is said that your dreams will come true if you make a wish to a shooting star.
>
> 聽說如果你向流星許願，你的願望就能成真。

Common Sense 小常識

美國的交通

美國人在外出時，通常首選的交通工具就是飛機，因此美國的機場算得上是最忙碌的，有時甚至在一分鐘內就同時有幾架飛機起飛或降落。

美國幾乎是人手一部私家車，一家人中無論是丈夫、妻子還是孩子，都有各自的車，因此美國石油消耗量世界第一也不足為奇了。

由於飛機和私家車的普及，美國的公車上乘客比較少，基本隨時都有空位，不會有人站著乘車，也絕不會出現超載的現象，這與台灣都市的公共交通系統大相逕庭。

美國的火車大多是沿著山區峽谷或沿海風景區行走，因此速度非常慢，價格卻又非常昂貴，這點也跟台灣十分不同，美國人的首選交通工具不是火車，而是又快又便宜的飛機。

Key Sentences 基本句大變身

track036

1	I'm stuck in a traffic jam.	我遇到塞車了。

- I was caught in traffic jam.
  我遇到塞車了。
- Traffic has come to a dead stop.
  交通已處於停滯狀態。

2	Traffic was interrupted by a dense fog.	交通因濃霧而受阻。

- The heavy snow blocked all roads.
  大雪阻塞了所有道路。
- The dense fog caused the traffic jam.
  濃霧導致了交通堵塞。

3	Traffic jam is a common occurrence.	塞車是很常見的事。

- The traffic is always in a state of confusion.
  交通情況總是很混亂。
- Traffic reaches a peak at this time of day.
  每天的這個時間是交通尖峰時刻。

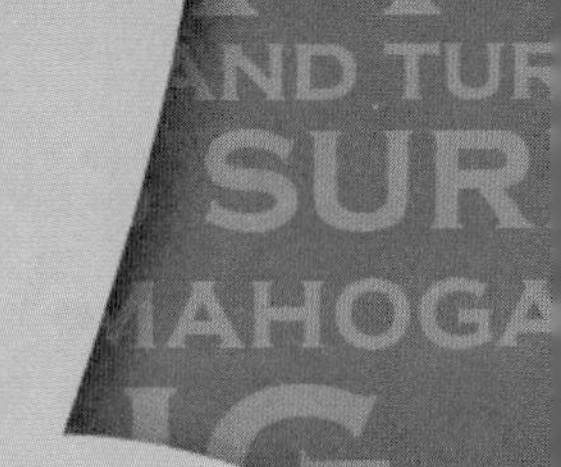

Chapter 3

Diet

用餐事宜篇

14 Reserving a Restaurant 預訂餐廳

Dialogue 1 第一次聊就上手

track037

Hostess : Can I help you?
Lily : Yes. I'd like to reserve a table for dinner.
Hostess : How large a group are you expecting?
Lily : Four people.
Hostess : Would you like to reserve a private dinning room?
Lily : That sounds like a good idea.
Hostess : All right. May I know your name, please?
Lily : Certainly. My name is Lily Smith.
Hostess: What time will you be arriving?
Lily : Around 5:30 pm.
Hostess : All right. We have reserved a private dining room for you at 5:30 pm. Thank you for calling.
Lily : Thank you very much.

Translation 中譯照過來

服務生：我能幫您什麼嗎？
莉　莉：是的，我想要預訂晚餐的位子。
服務生：你們會來多少個人？
莉　莉：四個人。
服務生：您願意預訂包廂嗎？
莉　莉：聽起來是個好主意。
服務生：好的，能告訴我您的名字嗎？
莉　莉：當然。我叫莉莉 ・ 史密斯。
服務生：您們什麼時候來？
莉　莉：下午五點半左右。
服務生：好的。我們已經為您預訂了一間下午五點半的包廂。感謝您的來電。
莉　莉：非常感謝。

Key words 重點單字快速記

hostess [ˋhostɪs] 名. （美國餐廳裡的）女服務生
reserve [rɪˋzɝv] 動. 預訂
dinner [ˋdɪnɚ] 名. 晚餐
expect [ɪkˋspɛkt] 動. 預期
private [ˋpraɪvɪt] 形. 安靜的，人不多的

Patterns 延伸句型快速學

01 ***S + would like to + V.***

（……想要……。）

I would like to have a glass of water.
我想要一杯水。

02 ***That sounds like ....***

（聽起來……。）

This sounds like a great plan.
聽起來是個好計畫。

Common Sense 小常識

美國餐館

美國的餐館包羅萬象，人們可以品嚐到世界各地的美食。最常見的有披薩店、中餐館、韓國餐館、壽司店和印度餐館，還有麥當勞和肯德基等速食店。因此，美國人不用走出國門就能吃遍天下。

14 Reserving a Restaurant 預訂餐廳

Dialogue 2 第一次聊就上手

track038

Hostess : This is Century Hotel. How can I help you?

Ella : I'd like to order a table for five this Saturday.

Hostess : All right. When would you like your table?

Ella : At around 5:30 pm.

Hostess : OK. May I have your name?

Ella : Sure. Ella Green, a table for five at about 5:30 this Saturday evening.

Translation 中譯照過來

服務生：這裡是世紀飯店，請問您有什麼需要？

艾　拉：我想訂一張這週六的五人餐桌。

服務生：好的。您什麼時候需要？

艾　拉：大約下午 5:30。

服務生：好的。能告訴我您的名字嗎？

艾　拉：當然。艾拉 ・ 格林，這週六晚上 5:30，一張五個人的餐桌。

Key words 重點單字快速記

hotel [hoˋtɛl] 名. 飯店
order [ˋɔrdɚ] 動. 訂；點
table [ˋtebl̩] 名. 桌子
Saturday [ˋsætɚde] 名. 星期六
around [əˋraʊnd] 形. 大約

Patterns 延伸句型快速學

01 *... at around* + 時間 .

（……大約……。）

> The meeting began at around 11 o'clock this morning.
> 會議大約是今天早上 11 點開始。

02 *... at about* + 時間 .

（……大約……。 ）

> It started to rain at about 6 this morning.
> 雨大約是今天早上 6 點開始下的。

Common Sense 小常識

美國餐館

雖然美國是個美食的大雜燴天堂，但是大部分在美國當地的外來食物，口味、分量等都已經有經過改良，被製作成更加符合美國人文化及口味的食物，例如超級甜的糖醋雞塊、顏色繽紛並加上一堆醬料的「美式」壽司捲，都是很好的例子！

Key Sentences 基本句大變身

track039

1	I'd like to reserve a table for three at 7 pm, please.	我想預訂下午七點的一張三人桌。

- I'd like to book a table for a party of five at 7 pm, please.
  我想預訂一張下午 7 點的五人桌來聚餐。
- I'd like to book a table for three at 6 pm in the name of John, please.
  我想以約翰的名義訂一張下午六點的三人桌。

2	Could we have a table by the window, please?	我們能要一張靠窗的桌子嗎？

- Could we have a non-smoking table, please?
  我們可以要一張無菸區的桌子嗎？
- Could we have a table away from the kitchen / toilets, please?
  我們可以要一張遠離廚房／廁所的桌子嗎？

3	I'm sorry. We're all booked up tonight.	抱歉，今天晚上都訂滿了。

- I'm sorry. We are quite full tonight.
  抱歉，今晚都訂滿了。
- I'm sorry. All the tables are booked tonight.
  抱歉，今晚的桌位已經都被預訂了。

4	How long is the wait?	要等多長時間？

- How long do we have to wait?
  我們要等多長時間？
- Is the wait long?
  要等很久嗎？

15 Ordering a Meal 點餐

Dialogue 1 第一次聊就上手

track040

Waiter : Can I help you, Sir?

Tom : Can you recommend me a delicious hamburger?

Waiter : Of course. Do you like hot food or light food?

Tom : I like light food.

Waiter : Then I will recommend the Mini Burger Combo. It's delicious.

Tom : All right. I'll take this one.

Waiter : OK.

Translation 中譯照過來

服務員：需要幫助嗎，先生？

湯　姆：你可以幫我推薦一款可口的漢堡嗎？

服務員：當然了。您喜歡吃辣的還是清淡的？

湯　姆：我喜歡吃清淡的。

服務員：那我建議您來個迷你綜合堡。味道很棒。

湯　姆：好的。我就點這個。

服務員：好的。

recommend [ˌrɛkəˋmɛnd] 動. 推薦，介紹
delicious [dɪˋlɪʃəs] 形. 美味的，可口的
hamburger [ˋhæmbɝgɚ] 名. 漢堡
light [laɪt] 形. 清淡的；不膩的
food [fud] 名. 食物

Patterns 延伸句型快速學

01 ***Can you recommend...?***

（你能推薦……嗎？）

> Can you recommend me a good novel?
> 你能推薦我一本好小說嗎？

02 ***Sb will take sth.***

（某人就要某物。）

> A：Which pen do you want, red or brown?
> B：Ummm, I will take the brown one.
> A：你想要哪支筆，紅色還是咖啡色？B：嗯……，我就要咖啡色的。

Common Sense 小常識

在美國點餐

在美國，菜單上通常很少會有圖片展示，但是每道菜的成分和製作方式卻寫得清清楚楚，既方便客人依個人口味選擇食物，也避免造成客人點到易過敏的食物。點餐時，當你選好食物後只需把菜單闔上，服務生自然會過來詢問。

15 Ordering a Meal 點餐

Dialogue 2 第一次聊就上手

track041

Waiter : Can I take your order now?

Bonny : Yes. I'd like ham and eggs, please.

Waiter : How do you want your eggs?

Bonny : What are my choices?

Waiter : Scrambled, sunny side-up and over-easy.

Bonny : Scrambled, please.

Waiter : OK.

Translation 中譯照過來

服務員：現在點餐嗎？

邦　妮：是的，我想要火腿和雞蛋。

服務員：你想要怎樣的蛋呢？

邦　妮：有哪些選擇呢？

服務員：炒蛋、單面煎的和兩面煎的。

邦　妮：請給我炒蛋。

服務員：好的。

Key words 重點單字快速記

ham [hæm] 名. 火腿，火腿肉
egg [ɛg] 名. 蛋
choice [tʃɔɪs] 名. 選擇
scramble [`skræmbḷ] 動. 炒
sunny side-up egg [`sʌnɪ saɪd.ʌp ɛg]
名. 太陽蛋（煎單面）
over-easy egg [.ovɚ`izɪ ɛg] 名. 半生熟荷包蛋（煎兩面）

Patterns 延伸句型快速學

01 *Sb takes sb's order....*

（某人（協助）點餐。）

When the waitress took our order, she smiled at us and walked away.
當那位女服務生點完餐後，她對我們微笑並且走開。

02 *How do you want your sth?*

（您想要某物怎麼處理？）

How do you want your steak?
您想要牛排怎麼處理？

Common Sense 小常識

在美國點餐

千萬不要高舉手臂招呼服務生，這樣是很不禮貌的。你可以向他稍微點點頭或微笑示意。有時也會碰到服務生提前來詢問的情況，如果還沒準備好你可以說 "I need a few more minutes." 或者如果你有任何疑問，都可以在這時向服務生提出。

Key Sentences 基本句大變身

track042

1 Can I have a menu, please? 請給我菜單好嗎？

- May I see your menu, please? 我可以看一下你們的菜單嗎？
- I'd like to see a menu, please. 請給我看看菜單。

2 Do you have a menu in Chinese? 你們有中文的菜單嗎？

- May I see a menu in Chinese? 我能看看中文菜單嗎？
- Do you have a Chinese menu? 你們有中文菜單嗎？

3 May I take your order now? 現在可以點菜嗎？

- Are you ready to order now? 您準備好點菜了嗎？
- What will you have? 您想要吃什麼？

4 What do you recommend? 你有什麼可以推薦的嗎？

- What is your suggestion? 你有什麼建議？
- Do you have any specialties? 你們有什麼特色菜嗎？

5 How would you like your steak cooked? 你的牛肉要幾分熟的？

- How would you like your steak prepared? 你的牛排要幾分熟？
- How would you like it done? 你想要幾分熟的？

16 Discussing the Food 討論餐點

Dialogue 1 第一次聊就上手

track043

Cashier : How was the meal today?

Customer : We were a little disappointed at today's meal.

Cashier : Oh, I'm sorry to hear that. What's wrong with the food?

Customer : The meat is tough, and it has a strong flavor.

Cashier : I'm so sorry and I'll take your drinks and dessert off the bill.

Customer : Oh, that would be nice. Thank you.

Translation 中譯照過來

收銀員：今天這頓飯如何？

顧　客：我們對今天的飯菜有點失望。

收銀員：哦，聽到這個消息我很抱歉。飯菜有什麼問題嗎？

顧　客：肉太老了，而且味道很重。

收銀員：太抱歉了，今天您帳單上的飲料和甜點免費。

顧　客：噢，這還不錯。謝謝。

Key words 重點單字快速記

disappointed [ˌdɪsəˋpɔɪntɪd] 形. 失望的，沮喪的

meal [mil] 名. 餐點

tough [tʌf] 形. 咬不動的；老的

flavor [ˋflevɚ] 名. 味道

drink [drɪŋk] 名. 飲料 動. 喝

dessert [dɪˋzɝt] 名. 甜食，甜品

Patterns 延伸句型快速學

01 *Sb + be + a little disappointed at + sth.*

（某人對某物感到有點失望。）

> Linda was a little disappointed at the singer's performance.
>
> 琳達對那位歌手的表現感到有點失望。

02 *take A off B.*

（把 A 從 B 中拿走。）

> I'd like to buy this laptop if you can take 10% off the price.
>
> 我想要買下這台筆電，如果你可以打個 9 折給我。
>
> （＝把 10% 的價格從總價中移除）

Common Sense 小常識

美國的代表性食物

奶油夾心海綿蛋糕（Twinkies）：以奶油做夾心的海綿蛋糕。
玉米片派（Frito Pie）：玉米片、乳酪、辣椒配上莎莎醬、豆泥、優酪乳油、大米和墨西哥辣椒等。
玉米熱狗（Corn Dogs）：香腸裹上玉米粉團，然後油炸即可。
巨無霸漢堡（Big Mac）：兩層或三層麵包中間夾著牛肉、乳酪、生菜等七種食物。
鄉村炸牛排（Chicken Fried Steak）：將調味後的麵粉裹到牛排上，然後進行煎炸。

16 Discussing the Food 討論餐點

Dialogue 2 第一次聊就上手

track044

Cathy : I can't eat anymore. What about you?

Mary : Me, too.

Cathy : I bring you here because this is my favorite restaurant.

Mary : Thank you very much. The food here is really delicious.

Cathy : How about having some desserts? The pudding here is great.

Mary : Yes, please.

Translation 中譯照過來

凱茜：我吃不下了。你呢？

瑪麗：我也是。

凱茜：我帶你來這裡是因為這是我最喜歡的餐廳。

瑪麗：非常感謝你。這裡的飯菜真的很美味。

凱茜：來點些甜點怎麼樣？這裡的布丁很棒。

瑪麗：好的。

Key words 重點單字快速記

anymore [ˋɛnɪmɔr] 副. 再也不

bring [brɪŋ] 動. 帶領

because [bɪˋkɔz] 連. 因為

favorite [ˋfevərɪt] 形. 最喜歡的

restaurant [ˋrɛstərənt] 名. 餐廳

pudding [ˋpudɪŋ] 名. 布丁

Patterns 延伸句型快速學

01 *...not...anymore.*

（不能再……。）

> I've worked for 18 hours and I can't work anymore.
> 我已經工作了 18 個小時，我不能再繼續工作了。

02 *S + V (+ O) because S + V (+ O).*

（……，因為……。）

> Peter got excellent grades on his final exam because he studied hard.
> 彼得在期末考拿到好成績，因為他唸書唸得很認真。

Common Sense 小常識

美國的代表性食物

噴霧乳酪（Spray Cheese）：一種可以用來烹飪食物的噴嘴式乳酪，對著食物噴抹即可。

油炸奶油（Deep Fried Butter）：看起來類似於炸鮮奶，曾榮獲「最具創意食物獎」。

午餐肉（SPAM）：在火腿（ham）中加入香料（spices）製成的罐頭食物。

火鴨雞三層肉（Turducken）：Turkey-duck-chicken 的合拼詞，就是在火雞肚子裡塞一隻鴨子，然後在鴨子肚子裡塞一隻雞，最後在雞肚子裡塞些燻肉和香腸，放到鍋裡油炸 2-3 小時即可。

Key Sentences 基本句大變身

track045

1 It smells good. 聞起來真香。

- It smells nice.
  聞起來很棒。
- It looks great!
  看起來真好吃！

2 It's good. 好吃。

- It's delicious.
  很美味。
- It's yummy.
  很美味。

3 It tastes strange. 味道很怪。

- This tastes funny.
  這味道很奇怪。
- This tastes weird.
  這味道很奇怪。

4 This bread is soggy. 麵包沒烤透。

- These potato chips are stale.
  馬鈴薯片味道怪怪的。
- This milk is sour.
  牛奶酸了。

5 It's salty. 真鹹。

- It's sweet / crispy / slimy / sour.
  真甜／脆／黏／酸。
- It's hot / spicy.
  真辣。

17 Paying the Check 買單

Dialogue 1 第一次聊就上手

track046

Lucy : It's my treat today.

Jerry : Why? It's on me.

Lucy : But you paid last time. Please let me pay this time.

Jerry : Don't worry about that. You can pay next time.

Lucy : All right.

Translation 中譯照過來

露西：今天我請客。

傑瑞：為什麼？我請客。

露西：但是你上一次請了，這次讓我請。

傑瑞：不用擔心。你可以下次請客。

露西：好吧。

Key words 重點單字快速記

treat [trit] 名. 款待，招待 動. 請客，款待，招待
pay [pe] 動. 支付
last [læst] 形. 上一次的
worry [ˋwɝɪ] 動. 擔心
next [nɛkst] 副. 下次

Patterns 延伸句型快速學

01 *Please let me V ....*

（請讓我……。）

To show my apology, please let me buy you a drink.

為了表達我的歉意，請讓我請你這杯飲料。

02 *Don't worry about + N.*

（不用擔心……。）

Don't worry about my condition. I already went to see the doctor.

不用擔心我的情況。我已經去看過醫生了。

Common Sense 小常識

宴席上的注意事項

與美國人一起用餐要注意以下幾點：

不抽煙、不說讓人作嘔之事、不寬衣解帶、不勸酒、不替他人夾菜、口中有食物時不出聲。

17 Paying the Check 買單

Dialogue 2 第一次聊就上手

track047

Waiter: Are you ready to go?

Wife: Yes, we are ready. What a nice dinner!

Husband: May I have the check, please?

Waiter: Certainly. I'll be right back with that. Here you are, sir.

Husband: Thank you.

Wife: Honey, don't forget the tip has already been added.

Translation 中譯照過來

服務員：您準備離開了嗎？

妻　子：是的，我們準備要走了。好棒的一頓晚餐！

丈　夫：請給我帳單，好嗎？

服務員：沒問題，我很快就來為您處理。先生，這是您的帳單。

丈　夫：謝謝。

妻　子：親愛的，別忘了帳單上已經額外加了小費。

ready [ˋrɛdɪ] 形. 準備好的
check [tʃɛk] 名. 帳單
certainly [ˋsɝtənlɪ] 副. 沒問題
forget [fɚˋgɛt] 動. 忘記
tip [tɪp] 名. 小費

Patterns 延伸句型快速學

01 *Are you ready to V ...?*

（你準備好要……了嗎？）

> Are you ready to accept the final challenge?
> 你準備好要接受最終挑戰了嗎？

02 *Don't forget (that) S + V (+ O).*

（不要忘記……。）

> Don't forget (that) you have an appointment with the dentist tomorrow.
> 不要忘記你明天跟牙醫有約。

Common Sense 小常識

宴席上的注意事項

在美國例如感恩節、聖誕節的大節日，美國的家庭會聚在一起分享美好的食物。而在美國的家庭宴席上，通常不會幫每個人分好菜，而是用大盆子或大餐盤盛裝食物，以傳遞的方式讓每個人夾取自己所需的分量。

Key Sentences 基本句大變身

track048

1 I'd like the check, please. 請幫我結帳。

- Could I have the check, please?
  請給我帳單，好嗎？
- Check, please.
  請結帳。

2 It is my treat. 我請客。

- It's on me.
  我請客。
- I'll treat you.
  我請你。

3 What is this charge for? 這個費用是什麼？

- What is this amount for?
  這是什麼的錢？
- What is this for?
  這錢是什麼的？

4 Let's go Dutch. 我們各付各的吧。

- Let's pay separately.
  我們各付各的吧。
- Let's divide the cost.
  我們分攤費用吧。

5 I'm afraid there is a mistake here. 我覺得這裡算錯了。

- I am afraid the check is incorrect.
  我怕帳單有錯。

KNESS—A T IN
D FOR THE BEDSIDE LAMP AND TURNED IT
UINTING AT HIS SURROU
S, AND A COLOSSAL MAHOGANY FO
ILIAR RING. PI
ROOM WITH LOUIS XVI FURE, HAND-FRE S
SCOUR-POSTER BED.LA N
HONE WAS RINGING IN THE A
D FOR THE BEDSIDE LAMP AND TURNED IT
UINTING AT HIS SURROU
S, AND A COLOSSAL MAHOGANY FO
ROOM WITH LOUIS XVI FURE, HAND-FRE S
SCOUR-POSTER BED.LA N
IDE TABLE.TH
ON A CRUMPLED FLYER ON
OUDLY PRESENTSA
DON PROFESSOR O
Y. A VISITOR? HIS EYES FOC
BCAN UNIVERSITY OF
RIN EVENING
GIOUS SYMBOLOGY, HARV
NIVERSITY LANGDO

Chapter 4

Love
愛情篇

18 Having a Crush 萌生愛意

Dialogue 1 第一次聊就上手

track049

Tom : Hey, Jerry, is Monica coming with us?

Jerry : Yes. Why?

Tom : Nothing. I'm just asking.

Jerry : Just asking? But why do you blush like that? Ah-huh, someone has a crush on Monica, doesn't he?

Tom : Who has a crush?

Jerry : Come on, Tom. Don't be such a chicken. If you like her, you've got to tell her. Maybe she likes you.

Tom : Well, I don't have the guts to ask her out.

Translation 中譯照過來

湯姆：嗨，傑瑞。莫妮卡會跟我們一起嗎？

傑瑞：是的。怎麼了？

湯姆：沒什麼，我只是問問。

傑瑞：只是問問？那為什麼你的臉紅成那樣？啊哈，有人迷戀上莫妮卡了，是吧？

湯姆：誰迷戀了？

傑瑞：行了吧，湯姆，別做膽小鬼了。如果你喜歡她就應該告訴她。可能她也喜歡你呢。

湯姆：但我沒有勇氣約她出來。

Key words 重點單字快速記

with [wɪð] 介. 一起
blush [blʌʃ] 動. （因難為情而）臉紅
crush [krʌʃ] 名. 迷戀，癡情；熱戀的對象，癡情的對象
chicken [ˋtʃɪkɪn] 名. 小雞；引申為膽小鬼，懦夫
ask [æsk] 動. 詢問

Patterns 延伸句型快速學

01 ***S + have / has a crush + on + ...***
（某人迷戀……。）

> Peter has a crush on his friend, Julia.
> 彼得迷戀他的朋友茱莉亞

02 ***Don't be such a + N.***
（別做……。）

> Don't be such a coward.
> 別做懦夫。

Common Sense 小常識

美國人如何看待「早戀」

其實在美國基本上不存在「早戀」這個詞，即便是十幾歲的孩子談戀愛也被看做是再正常不過的現象。美國父母會藉這個機會對孩子進行性教育，以此來預防性疾病和早孕問題。與此相反，亞洲地區的父母和老師通常會對「早戀」進行嚴厲的打擊，但在這樣的打擊下仍然會有生米煮成熟飯的情況發生，因此，加強對孩子的性教育對於父母來說變得尤為重要。

Key Sentences 基本句大變身

track050

1 She is so beautiful. 她太漂亮了。

■ she is so pretty.
她太漂亮了。

■ Lily is attractive.
莉莉很迷人。

2 I think he is cute. 我覺得他很可愛迷人。

■ He is lovely.
他很可愛。

■ He is cool.
他很有魅力。

3 She is really my type. 她真是我喜歡的類型。

■ He is a boy of my dreams.
他是我的夢中情人。

■ I want to date with her.
我想和她約會。

4 Kevin is really a lady-killer. 凱文真是個女性殺手。

■ Kevin turns every girl on.
凱文使每個女孩小鹿亂撞。

5 I fall in love with Lily. 我愛上了莉莉。

■ I have a crush on Lily.
我迷戀上了莉莉。

■ I'm head over heels in love with John.
我徹底愛上了約翰。

19 Confession 表白

Dialogue 1 第一次聊就上手

track051

Blair : Jack, why are you always being so nice to me?

Jack : Listen, I don't want to scare you, but I think I really fall in love with you.

Blair : Oh, oh my God...

Jack : I'm serious. Do you want to be my girlfriend?

Blair : You are a good guy. I like you. But I think I need more time...

Jack : Oh, that's OK.

Translation 中譯照過來

布蕾兒：傑克，你為什麼總是對我這麼好？

傑　克：聽著，我不想嚇到你，但我覺得我真的愛上了你。

布蕾兒：噢，噢我的天呀⋯⋯

傑　克：我是認真的。你想做我的女朋友嗎？

布蕾兒：你是個好人，我喜歡你，但我覺得我需要更多的時間⋯⋯

傑　克：哦，沒有關係。

Key words 重點單字快速記

nice [naɪs] 形. 好的

scare [skɛr] 動. 使驚恐，嚇唬

serious [`sɪrɪəs] 形. 嚴肅的，認真的

girlfriend [`gɝl͵frɛnd] 名. 女朋友；女性朋友

guy [gaɪ] 名. 男人，傢伙

Patterns 延伸句型快速學

01 ***S + be + always + being + adj. +....***

（某人總是⋯⋯。）

> He is always being great.
> 他總是表現很好。

02 ***S + fall / falls / fell in love + with + sb.***

（某人愛上某人。）

> She fell in love with her tutor.
> 她愛上了她的家教。

Common Sense 小常識

喜歡一個人怎麼辦

美國男女不管通過什麼方式認識後，如果男方對女方感興趣，通常會通過朋友或其他方式要到女方的電話。接下來就是單獨約女孩出來了。

19 Confession 表白

Dialogue 2 第一次聊就上手

track052

Daniel : Emily, I want to ask you a question and I hope you can answer it honestly. OK?

Emily : Go ahead.

Daniel : What do you think of me?

Emily : I think you're sincere, brave, handsome…

Daniel : You know I really care about you. I miss you so much these days. I love you…

Emily : I…

Translation 中譯照過來

丹尼爾：艾米麗，我想問你個問題，希望你能誠實地回答，好嗎？

艾米麗：問吧。

丹尼爾：你覺得我怎麼樣？

艾米麗：我覺得你誠懇、勇敢、帥氣……

丹尼爾：你知道的，我真的很在乎你。這些天我太想你了。我愛你……

艾米麗：我……

Key words 重點單字快速記

honestly [ˋɑnɪstlɪ] 副. 誠實地
sincere [sɪnˋsɪr] 形. 真誠的
brave [brev] 形. 勇敢的
handsome [ˋhænsəm] 形. 帥氣的
miss [mɪs] 動. 想念

Patterns 延伸句型快速學

01 ***S + hope / hopes (that) ....***
（某人希望……。）

I hope that it won't rain tomorrow.
我希望明天不會下雨。

02 ***What + aux. + S + think of + ...?***
（某人認為……如何？）

What does John think of our teacher?
約翰認為我們老師如何？

Common Sense 小常識

喜歡一個人怎麼辦

如果感覺機會太小，還可以求助朋友，多舉辦幾次活動，時間長了自然會熟悉一些。之後可以約女孩出來看電影、吃飯或者喝咖啡，但屬於非正式的約會。

Key Sentences 基本句大變身

track053

1 I need to talk to you. 我要跟你談談。

- Can we talk?
  我們能談談嗎？
- I would like to talk with you.
  我有話要跟你說。

2 Do you have a boyfriend / girlfriend now? 你現在有男／女朋友嗎？

- Are you dating anybody now?
  你目前在和誰約會嗎？
- Are you seeing anyone now?
  你現在在和誰交往嗎？

3 What do you think of me? 你覺得我怎麼樣？

- What do you think about me?
  你認為我怎麼樣？

4 I love you. 我愛你。

- I'm in love with you.
  我愛著你。
- I fall in love with you.
  我愛上你了。

20 Falling in Love 戀愛

Dialogue 1 第一次聊就上手

track054

Stefan : Dear Elena, I love you.

Elena : I love you, too.

Stefan : I think we are made for each other.

Elena : Are you really thinking of that?

Stefan : Yes. I am so lucky to have met you.

Elena : I am happy to hear you say that.

Translation 中譯照過來

斯蒂芬：親愛的愛琳娜，我愛你。

愛琳娜：我也愛你。

斯蒂芬：我覺得我們是天生的一對。

愛琳娜：你真的這樣想嗎？

斯蒂芬：是的。我真幸運遇見了你。

愛琳娜：我很高興聽到你這樣說。

Key words 重點單字快速記

dear [dɪr] 形. 親愛的
love [lʌv] 動. 愛
lucky [ˋlʌkɪ] 形. 運氣好的，幸運的
happy [ˋhæpɪ] 形.（使人感到）愉快的，幸福的
hear [hɪr] 動. 聽

Patterns 延伸句型快速學

01 *S + be made for + ...*

（為了……而打造。）

> These shoes are made for basketball players.
> 這些鞋是為籃球員而打造的。

02 *S + be + so + adj. + to V.*

（某人非常……去做……。）

> I am so glad to work with you.
> 我非常榮幸能與您一起共事。

Common Sense 小常識

正式約會

如果有一天一個美國男人跟你說：“Can I ask you out for a dinner?（我可以約你出去吃飯嗎？）”你一定要記得問一聲：“Is this a DATE?（這是個約會嗎？）”得到對方肯定的回答後，證明這就是一次正式的約會了。

20 Falling in Love 戀愛

Dialogue 2 第一次聊就上手

track055

Elena : Will you love me forever?

Stefan : I will, I promise.

Elena : Are you serious?

Stefan : Of course. Only by staying with you can make me happy.

Elena : Will we stay with each other forever?

Stefan : Yes. I would like to spend the rest of my life with you.

Translation 中譯照過來

愛琳娜：你會永遠愛我嗎？

斯蒂芬：我會的，我發誓。

愛琳娜：你是認真的嗎？

斯蒂芬：當然。只有跟你在一起我才開心。

愛琳娜：我們會永遠在一起嗎？

斯蒂芬：會的。我願與你共度餘生。

Key words 重點單字快速記

forever [fɚˋɛvɚ] 副. 永遠；長久地
promise [ˋprɑmɪs] 動. 保證，答應
stay [ste] 動. 停留
spend [spɛnd] 動. 花費
life [laɪf] 名. 生命

Patterns 延伸句型快速學

01 ***make + O + adj.***
（讓某人／某物感到……。）

My son makes me proud.
我兒子令我感到驕傲。

02 ***S + spend + N / Ving.***
（某人花費……。）

She spent half her savings to buy that purse.
她花了一半的積蓄去買那個皮包。

Common Sense 小常識

正式約會

與亞洲人戀愛最大的不同就是，美國人追女孩通常會到非常昂貴的餐館吃飯，雙方也會精心打扮一番，紅酒配佳人，非常正式。

Key 基本句大變身 Sentences

track056

1 Do you want to go out with me tonight? 今晚你能和我約會嗎？

- Let's go out tonight.
  今晚出去吧。
- Why don't we go out tonight?
  今晚我們為什麼不出去走走呢？

2 May I ask you out? 我能約你出去嗎？

- Would you mind if I took you out?
  你介意我約你出去嗎？
- Would you go on a date with me?
  你願意和我約會嗎？

3 Will you love me forever? 你會永遠愛我嗎？

- Are you serious with me?
  你對我是認真的嗎？

4 I'm happy to have known you. 能認識你我很幸福。

- You make me happy.
  你讓我覺得很幸福。
- I can feel your kindness.
  我能感覺到你的好。

21 Quarreling & Breaking Up 吵架和分手

Dialogue 1 第一次聊就上手

track057

David : Hi, Jack. Haven't seen you for a while. How is Daisy?

Jack : We're not seeing each other anymore.

David : What happened? Did you break up?

Jack : Yeah. I am tired of her nagging all the time.

David : Oh, I'm sorry to hear that.

Translation 中譯照過來

大衛：嗨，傑克。好久沒見你了。黛西怎麼樣？

傑克：我們已經不再見面了。

大衛：發生什麼事了？你們分手了？

傑克：是的。我厭倦了她不斷的嘮叨。

大衛：噢，聽到這個我很抱歉。

Key words 重點單字快速記

while [hwaɪl] 名. 一段時間
happen [ˋhæpən] 動. 發生
tired [taɪrd] 形. 疲倦的
nagging [ˋnægɪŋ] 名. 叨嘮
sorry [ˋsɑrɪ] 形. 抱歉的

Patterns 延伸句型快速學

01 ***...not... any more.***
（已不再……。）

Chris is not one of the team members any more.
克里斯已不再是隊員了。

02 ***S + be + tired of + Ving / N.***
（某人厭倦……。）

Emma is tired of her husband's lies.
艾瑪已經厭倦了她丈夫的謊言。

Common Sense 小常識

美國人的戀愛觀（1）

美國人戀愛找的是靈魂伴侶（soul mate），他們更看重性格（personality）、共同興趣（common interests）、性傾向（sexuality）和對事物的共同看法和觀點（similar values and norms）。雙方從第一次約會（the first date）開始，談論彼此對人生、愛情的看法，如果合得來，就會繼續約會，但在約會期間彼此只是朋友關係，只要沒有確定戀愛關係，雙方都可以與其他人約會。

21 Quarreling & Breaking Up 吵架和分手

Dialogue 2 第一次聊就上手

track058

Damon : Hi, Tyler, we're having a party tonight. Wanna come join us? You can bring your girlfriend.

Tyler : Well...I'm breaking up with Lucy.

Damon : What happened? Did you have a fight?

Tyler : No. She's really a very nice girl. But sometimes she's too caring...well...no...she's just possessive...and...uh...I kind of want a break...you know...for some room for myself.

Damon : Did you talk with her about it?

Tyler : I've tried, but it didn't work.

Damon : I know she's head over heels in love with you. She'll be badly hurt!

Tyler : I know...

Translation 中譯照過來

戴蒙：嗨，泰勒。今晚我們有個聚會，想要加入我們嗎？你可以帶上你的女朋友。

泰勒：嗯……我要和露西分手了。

戴蒙：發生什麼事了？你們吵架了？

泰勒：沒有。她真的是個好女孩。但有時候她管得太多了……嗯……不……她是佔有欲太強了……而且……嗯……我有點想分手……你知道的……給自己點空間。

戴蒙：你跟她談過這些了嗎？

泰勒：我試過了，但不起作用。

戴蒙：我知道，她太愛你了，會受傷很深的。

泰勒：我知道……

Key words 重點單字快速記

fight [faɪt] 動. 爭吵，爭論

possessive [pəˋzɛsɪv]

形.（愛情／友情）佔有欲強的，自私的

myself [maɪˋsɛlf] 代. 我自己

try [traɪ] 動. 嘗試

hurt [hɝt] 動. 傷害（感情），（使）傷心

Patterns 延伸句型快速學

01 *S + kind of + V....*

（某人有點……。）

Hamilton kind of got a chance to ask Christine out, but he screwed up.

漢彌爾頓有點有機會約克莉絲丁出去約會，但他搞砸了。

02 *S + be + head over heels in love with ....*

（某人深愛上某人。）

I am head over heels in love with Lynn.

我深深愛著琳。

Common Sense 小常識

美國人的戀愛觀（2）

美國人選擇戀人時在年齡上沒有過多的要求，只要雙方合得來就好。但這並不意味著越年輕漂亮越好。美國男人認為年齡差距過於懸殊，彼此之間可能會缺少共同語言，因此，普通美國人的生活中很少有老夫少妻。

Key Sentences 基本句大變身

track059

1 I've had enough of you. 我受夠你了。

■ I'm fed up with you.
我對你厭倦了。

2 I think we should break up. 我想我們應該分手。

■ Let's part.
我們分手吧。

■ I want to break up with you.
我想和你分手。

3 I'm tired of fighting with you. 我厭倦了跟你吵架。

■ We keep fighting a lot, and I feel so tired.
我們時常打架，我感覺太累。

4 Please give me another chance. 請再給我一次機會。

■ Can you forgive me?
你能原諒我嗎？

■ Will you give me a chance?
你能給我一次機會嗎？

22 Proposal 求婚

Dialogue 1 第一次聊就上手

track060

Ross: Dear Rachel, I love you.

Rachel: I love you, too.

Ross: I want to protect you forever. Will you marry me?

Rachel: Oh, God! Are you serious?

Ross: Am I too abrupt? Did I scare you? Or you don't want...

Rachel: No! No! I have been expecting this moment for a long time. I mean my answer is "Yes."

Ross: Oh, I'm so happy. I will try my best to take care of you. I promise.

Rachel: We'll be happy.

Translation 中譯照過來

羅　斯：親愛的瑞吉兒，我愛你。

瑞吉兒：我也愛你。

羅　斯：我想永遠保護你，嫁給我好嗎？

瑞吉兒：噢，天啊！你是認真的嗎？

羅　斯：是不是我太唐突了？嚇到你了嗎？還是你不想……

瑞吉兒：不是！不是的！我已經期盼這一刻很久了。我想說我的答案是「我願意」。

羅　斯：噢，我太高興了。我會好好照顧你的，我向你承諾。

瑞吉兒：我們會幸福的。

Key words 重點單字快速記

proposal [prə`pozḷ] 名. 求婚
protect [prə`tɛkt] 動. 保護
marry [`mærɪ] 動. 結婚；娶；嫁
abrupt [ə`brʌpt] 形. 粗魯的，生硬的
moment [`momənt] 名. 時刻
promise [`prɑmɪs] 動. 承諾

Patterns 延伸句型快速學

01 *S + have / has + been + Ving....*

（某人已經……。）

Students have been craving for the four consecutive holidays for a long time.
學生們已渴望四天連假許久。

02 *Sb + try sb's best + to V.*

（某人盡力做到……。）

Usian Bolt tried his best to win the gold medal.
波爾特盡他最大的努力贏得金牌。

Common Sense 小常識

求婚

在美國，男生求婚之前，需要得到女生父親的同意（permission），所以有些女生在聽到男朋友的求婚時，第一反應不是回答 Yes 或 No，而是問：「你問過我父親了是吧？你得到他的同意了嗎？」

Key 基本句大變身 Sentences

track061

1	Will you marry me?	你願意嫁給我嗎？

- Would you like to be my partner in life?
  你願意做我的人生伴侶嗎？
- Let's get married.
  我們結婚吧。

2	I want to spend the rest of my life with you.	我想和你共度餘生。

- Would you like to be my wife?
  你願意做我的妻子嗎？
- I love you with all my heart.
  我全心全意地愛著你。

3	Yes, I would like to marry you.	我願意嫁給你。

- Yes, I do.
  是的，我願意。
- I have been expecting this moment for a long time.
  我已經等這一刻好久了。

4	I don't want to marry against my will.	我不想違背自己的意願去結婚。

- I don't want to rush into marriage.
  我不想倉促結婚。

23 Getting Married 結婚

Dialogue 1 第一次聊就上手

track062

Lucy : Lily, what do you think of the wedding?

Lily : It's beautiful. I want to have a wedding like that.

Lucy : Do you like a big wedding like that?

Lily : No. I prefer a small wedding.

Lucy : But I like my wedding to be big and memorable.

Lily : Well, it's a matter of personal taste.

Translation 中譯照過來

露西：莉莉，你覺得婚禮怎麼樣？

莉莉：很漂亮，我也想要一個那樣的婚禮。

露西：你也想要一個那樣盛大的婚禮？

莉莉：不，我更喜歡小型的婚禮。

露西：但我想要自己的婚禮又盛大又令人難忘。

莉莉：好吧，個人喜好不同。

Key words 重點單字快速記

wedding [ˋwɛdɪŋ] 名. 婚禮
beautiful [ˋbjutəfəl] 形. 美麗的
memorable [ˋmɛmərəbl̩] 形. 難忘的，值得紀念的
personal [ˋpɝsn̩l̩] 形. 個人的，私人的
taste [test] 名. 口味

Patterns 延伸句型快速學

01 *I prefer ... than ....*

（我偏好……更甚於……。）

> As for the dessert, I prefer chocolate cake than ice cream.
> 至於甜點，我偏好巧克力蛋糕更甚於冰淇淋。

02 *It's a matter of + N.*

（這只是……的問題。）

> It's just a matter of time.
> 這只是時間的問題。

Common Sense 小常識

良辰吉日

跟台灣人一樣，美國人結婚也是要選擇良辰吉日的。大多數美國人喜歡在六月結婚，六月的英文是 June。在羅馬神話中，代表愛情和婚姻的女神名字叫做 Juno，而 June 正是取自於它。因此，美國人認為在六月舉行婚禮就可以得到愛情和婚姻女神的眷顧和祝福。

Key Sentences 基本句大變身

track063

1 When will you hold the wedding? 你們什麼時候舉辦婚禮？

- Where do you want the wedding to be held?
  你們想在哪裡舉行婚禮？
- Where will you hold the wedding?
  你們將在哪裡舉行婚禮？

2 Have you bought your wedding dress? 你買婚紗了嗎？

- Have you prepared food for the wedding?
  你為婚禮準備好食物了嗎？

3 The bride wore a white wedding dress. 新娘身著一身白色婚紗。

- The bride smiled happily.
  新娘幸福地微笑著。
- The bride and the bridegroom are a good match.
  新郎和新娘很速配。

4 I've been very happy since I married Jack. 和傑克結婚後我很幸福。

- I've been the happiest woman in the world since I married Jack.
  嫁給傑克我就成了世界上最幸福的女人。
- Thank you for being there for so many years, Jack.
  謝謝你多年來一直陪伴著我，傑克。

24 Getting Pregnant 懷孕

Dialogue 1 第一次聊就上手

track064

Alice : Honey, I've got good news for you.

Joey : What is it?

Alice : You are going to be a father.

Joey : What? Do you mean that you are pregnant?

Alice : Yes. We'll have our baby soon.

Joey : Oh, dear, I'm so happy.

Alice : Me, too.

Translation 中譯照過來

愛麗絲：親愛的，我有好消息要告訴你。

喬　伊：是什麼好消息呢？

愛麗絲：你要做爸爸了。

喬　伊：什麼？你的意思是你懷孕了？

愛麗絲：是的，我們很快就會有我們的寶寶了。

喬　伊：噢，親愛的，我太高興了。

愛麗絲：我也是。

Key words 重點單字快速記

pregnant [ˋprɛgnənt] 形 懷孕的，妊娠的
father [ˋfɑðɚ] 名 父親
mean [min] 名 意思
baby [ˋbebɪ] 名 寶寶
soon [sun] 副 很快地

Patterns 延伸句型快速學

01 *S + be going to + V.*
（即將……。）

> The next ship is going to arrive in 3 hours.
> 下一班船即將在三小時後抵達。

02 *Do you mean that ...?*
（你的意思是……嗎？）

> Do you mean that we are running out of gas?
> 你的意思是我們沒油了？

Common Sense 小常識

美國孕婦

美國孕婦平時除了做一些必要的防範措施外，其他一切生活基本上都會照舊。

飲食：忌菸酒，吃保健品，正餐與平時基本相同。

工作：正常上班。

家務：除特殊情況外，平時做什麼，懷孕後照樣做什麼。有的孕婦甚至會自己開割草機修剪草坪。

出行：開車、乘飛機、乘地鐵、騎自行車。

Key 基本句大變身 Sentences

track065

1 I'm pregnant. 我懷孕了。

- I'm having a baby.
  我有寶寶了。
- I'm expecting.
  我有身孕了。

2 How long have you been pregnant? 你懷孕多久了？

- How far pregnant are you?
  你懷孕多久了？

3 Do not smoke during pregnancy. 懷孕期間不要吸煙。

- Don't make your wife angry when she is pregnant.
  你不要在妻子懷孕期間惹她生氣。
- Take care of yourself.
  照顧好自己。

4 Congratulations! 恭喜你！

- I was ever so pleased to hear that you're expecting baby.
  聽說你懷孕了，我非常高興。

25 Giving Birth to a New Baby 新生命誕生

Dialogue 1 第一次聊就上手

track066

Chandler : Honey, what's wrong with you?

Monica : I feel very nervous.

Chandler : Take it easy. We are going to have our own baby. You should be happy.

Monica : Yeah, I know.

Chandler : The doctors and the nurses will help you. And I will be waiting for you right here, praying for you and our baby.

Monica : Thank you, honey. I feel better now.

Translation 中譯照過來

錢德勒：親愛的，你怎麼了？

莫妮卡：我很緊張。

錢德勒：放輕鬆。我們將要迎來我們自己的寶寶。你應該高興呀。

莫妮卡：是的，我知道。

錢德勒：醫生和護士都會幫助你的。我也會一直在這裡等你，為你和我們的寶寶祈禱。

莫妮卡：謝謝你，親愛的。我感覺好多了。

Key words 重點單字快速記

birth [bɝθ] 名. 出生；分娩
nervous [ˋnɝvəs] 形. 神經緊張的；焦慮不安的
own [on] 形. 自己的
pray [pre] 動. 祈禱
better [ˋbɛtɚ] 形. 更好的

Patterns 延伸句型快速學

01 *What's wrong with + sb / sth?*
（某人／某物怎麼了；某人／某物發生了什麼事了？）

> What's wrong with the little puppy?
> 小狗怎麼了？

02 *...Ving....*
（……，（而且）……。）

> The girl sat there, singing the song.
> 女孩坐在那兒，唱著歌。

Common Sense 小常識

美國女人不坐月子

大部分亞洲女人生完孩子後都會坐月子，第一個月裡不能吹風，不能洗頭髮，還要臥床，規矩相當多。但是在美國，媽媽生完孩子後只會休息一個星期甚至幾天，就會去上班，洗澡吹頭髮更是常有的事，對於美國女人來說，讓她們一個月不洗澡比登天還難。

Key Sentences 基本句大變身

track067

1	Have you made good preparation for the baby?	你為迎接寶寶做好準備了嗎？

- Have you prepared well for the baby?
  你準備好迎接寶寶了嗎？
- What have you prepared for the baby?
  你為寶寶做了些什麼準備？

2	When is the baby due?	預產期是什麼時候？

- I'm having a baby in June.
  我將在 6 月生孩子。
- My due date will be on June 15th.
  我的預產期是 6 月 15 日。

3	Do you have any name picked out for our baby?	你為我們的孩子取名字了嗎？

- I need to give our baby a good name.
  我應該給我們的孩子起個好名字。
- It's too difficult to think of a name for our baby.
  給我們的孩子取名字真是太難了。

4	The birth of the baby filled our family with joy.	寶寶的出生使我們的家庭充滿了快樂。

- Our whole family feels very happy because of the new baby.
  我們全家人都因為這個新生命而感到無比幸福。

KNESS—A T IN

O FOR THE BEDSIDE LAMP AND TURNED IT

UINTING AT HIS SURROU

S, AND A COLOSSAL MAHOGANY FO

ILIAR RING. P

ROOM WITH Louis XVI FURE, HAND-FRE S

SCOUR-POSTER BED.La N

HONE WAS RINGING IN THE A

O FOR THE BEDSIDE LAMP AND TURNED IT

UINTING AT HIS SURROU

S, AND A COLOSSAL MAHOGANY FO

ROOM WITH Louis XVI FURE, HAND-FRE S

SCOUR-POSTER BED.La N

IDE TABLE.TH

ON A CRUMPLED FLYER ON

OUDLY PRESENTSA

GDON PROFESSOR O

Y. A VISITOR? His EYES FOC

BCAN UNIVERSITY OF

RIN EVENING

GIOUS SYMBOLOGY, HARV

NIVERSITY LANGDO

Chapter 5

School Life

校園生活篇

26 Admissions 入學

Dialogue 1 第一次聊就上手

track068

Tom: It's a great day, isn't it?

Rose: Yes, it is. I'm Rose. Nice to meet you.

Tom: Nice to meet you, too. My name is Tom.

Rose: Are you a freshman?

Tom: Yes. How about you?

Rose: Me, too.

Tom: Great. Maybe we can study together. I think we can be good friends.

Rose: Yeah, anytime.

Translation 中譯照過來

湯姆：天氣很好，是吧？

羅絲：是的。我叫羅斯。很高興認識你。

湯姆：我也很高興認識你。我的名字叫湯姆。

羅絲：你是新生嗎？

湯姆：是的。你呢？

羅絲：我也是。

湯姆：太好了。也許我們可以一起學習。我想我們會成為很好的朋友的。

羅絲：是啊，隨時可以。

Key words 重點單字快速記

admission [əd`mɪʃən] 名. 錄取，錄用
freshman [`frɛʃmən] 名. （高中／大學）一年級新鮮人
maybe [`mebɪ] 副. 大概；或許
study [`stʌdɪ] 動. 念書
friend [frɛnd] 名. 朋友
anytime [`ɛnɪ͵taɪm] 副. 任何時候

Patterns 延伸句型快速學

01 ***Maybe S + V (+ O).***
（或許……。）

Maybe he is not that into you.
或許他沒那麼喜歡你。

02 ***S think (that) S + V (+ O).***
（某人認為……。）

Jennifer thinks that she is pretty.
珍妮佛覺得自己很漂亮。

Common Sense 小常識

常春藤大學聯盟

美國常春藤大學聯盟是由哈佛大學、耶魯大學、賓夕法尼亞大學、普林斯頓大學、哥倫比亞大學、布朗大學、達特茅斯大學、康乃爾大學組成的聯盟。這些大學無論是綜合實力、學術實力，還是教學實力，在世界上都名列前茅。

Key 基本句大變身 Sentences

track069

1 Where can I register? 哪裡可以註冊？

- Where is the infirmary?
  醫務室在哪裡？
- Could you tell me where the campus cafeteria is?
  你能告訴我學校食堂在哪裡嗎？

2 Who is your roommate? 你的室友是誰？

- Who are you rooming with?
  你和誰住同一個房間？

3 I like to live in the dormitory. 我喜歡住在宿舍裡。

- I'd like to rent an apartment.
  我想租一套公寓。
- I don't like to live with so many people.
  我不想和那麼多人住在一起。

4 This building has an elevator. 這棟樓裡有電梯。

- There is an elevator in this building.
  這棟樓裡有電梯。
- This building has security.
  這棟樓有保全措施。

27 Major Courses 專業課程

Dialogue 1 第一次聊就上手

track070

Rose : Excuse me. Can I ask some questions?

Students services manager : Certainly. What do you want to know?

Rose : Could you please tell me how many credits should I get for a bachelor's degree?

Students services manager : You have to get 200 credits, including required courses and optional courses.

Rose : OK. How long does it take to earn a bachelor's degree?

Students services manager : Four years.

Rose : OK. Thank you very much.

Students services manager : You're welcome.

Translation 中譯照過來

羅　　　　　斯：打擾一下。我可以問您一些問題嗎？

學生事務管理人員：當然。你想問什麼？

羅　　　　　斯：您能告訴我要多少學分才能拿到學士學位嗎？

學生事務管理人員：你必須得到 200 學分，包括必修課和選修課。

羅　　　　　斯：好的。那麼多長時間可以取得學士學位呢？

學生事務管理人員：4 年。

羅　　　　　斯：好的，非常感謝您。

學生事務管理人員：不客氣。

Key words 重點單字快速記

major [ˋmedʒɚ] 名.（大學）主修科目，專業
動.（在大學）主修

course [kors] 名. 課程

credit [ˋkrɛdɪt] 名. 學分

bachelor [ˋbætʃələ] 名. 學士

degree [dɪˋgri] 名. 學位；（大學）學位課程

required [rɪˋkwaɪrd] 形. 必修的（大學課程）

Patterns 延伸句型快速學

01 *Could you please tell me ...?*

（能請您告訴我……嗎？）

Could you please tell me what I should do to get your permission?

能請您告訴我該做些什麼以取得您的同意？

02 *..., including N.*

（……，包括……。）

Ten persons were killed in the explosion, including the two bombers.

有十人在那場爆炸中喪生，其中包括兩名炸彈客。

Common Sense 小常識

美國的課堂

在美國課堂上一定要積極參加課堂討論，因為很多老師是根據課堂表現給學生評分的，這些分數有時占了很大的比重。因此上課時，一定要積極發言。跟老師說話時要看著他的眼睛，抬頭挺胸。切忌總是低頭記筆記或者跟同桌說話。

Key Sentences 基本句大變身

track071

1 What's your major? 你的主修是什麼？

- What do you major in?
  你的主修是什麼？
- What subject do you major in?
  你的主修是什麼？

2 My major is English. 我的主修是英語。

- I major in English.
  我的主修是英語。
- I take English as my major.
  我的主修是英語。

3 How many credits should I get for a bachelor's degree? 我要達到多少學分才能拿到學士學位？

- How long does it take to earn a bachelor's degree?
  多長時間可以取得學士學位？

4 How many required courses do you have? 你有幾門必修課？

- How many optional courses do you have?
  你有幾門選修課？

28 In 在圖書館 the Library

Dialogue 1 第一次聊就上手

track072

Tom: Excuse me, sir? I want to apply for a library card. Can you help me?

Librarian : Yes. Please give me your ID card and a photo.

Tom : Here you are.

Librarian : You need to give me 10 dollars for the deposit. And the library card is free.

Tom : OK. Here is the money. And If I return the card, can I get the refund?

Librarian : Of course, as long as the card is well kept.

Translation 中譯照過來

湯　　　姆：打擾一下，先生。我想辦一張圖書證。你能幫我嗎？

圖書管理員：是的。請給我你的身分證和一張照片。

湯　　　姆：給你。

圖書管理員：你需要給我 10 美元作押金。圖書證是免費的。

湯　　　姆：好的。給你錢。那麼如果我退交圖書證，我可以取回押金嗎？

圖書管理員：當然可以了，只要你的圖書證保存完好。

Key words 重點單字快速記

library [ˋlaɪ͵brɛrɪ] 名. 圖書館
librarian [laɪˋbrɛrɪən] 名. 圖書館管理員
photo [ˋfoto] 名. 照片
deposit [dɪˋpɑzɪt] 名. (租用物品)押金;保證金
return [rɪˋtɝn] 動. 歸還
refund [ˋrɪ͵fʌnd] 名. 退款

Patterns 延伸句型快速學

01 *S apply for ....*

(某人申請……。)

> Cena wants to apply for UCLA.
> 希南想要申請加州大學洛杉磯分校。

02 *as long as ....*

(只要……,就……。)

> Olsen is not coming back to the team as long as Jess is still in.
> 只要傑西還在,歐森就不會歸隊。

Common Sense 小常識

最棒的美國大學圖書館

圖書館名稱	所在大學	地點	設立時間
Cook Legal Research Library	密西根大學	安娜堡市,密西根州	1931 年
William Oxley Thompson Memorial Library	俄亥俄州立大學	哥倫布市,俄亥俄州	1912 年
Linderman Library	理海大學	伯利恒市,賓夕法尼亞州	1878 年
Hale Library	堪薩斯州立大學	曼哈頓,堪薩斯州	1927 年
William R. Perkins Library	杜克大學	德罕,北卡羅來納州	1839 年
Harry Elkins Widener Memorial Library	哈佛大學	劍橋市,麻塞諸塞州	1915 年
Smathers Library	佛羅里達大學	蓋恩斯維爾,佛羅里達州	1926 年
Powell Library	加利福尼亞大學洛杉磯分校	洛杉磯,加利福尼亞州	1929 年
Wilson Library	北卡羅來納大學	教堂山,北卡羅來納州	1929 年
Thompson Memorial Library	瓦薩學院	波基普西,紐約州	1865 年

Key Sentences 基本句大變身

track073

1	I want to apply for a library card.	我想辦一張圖書證。

- Where can I get a library card?
  我去哪裡領圖書證？
- When can I get a library card?
  我什麼時候能領到圖書證？

2	We can return your deposit money if the library card is well kept.	如果圖書證保存完好，我們就可以退還押金。

- There's a refund when you return the library card.
  你退還圖書證的時候可以取回押金。

3	I'd like to borrow a book.	我想借一本書。

- I'd like to borrow some books from the library.
  我想從圖書館裡借幾本書。
- Can I take out a book?
  我可以借走一本書嗎？

4	I will return it on time.	我會按時歸還的。

- You must return these books within two months.
  你必須在兩個月內歸還這些書。
- I will return these books in one month.
  我會在一個月之內歸還這些書的。

29 In the Laboratory 在實驗室

Dialogue 1 第一次聊就上手

track074

Teacher : Have you read the instructions?

Joey : Yes. But it seems that there's something wrong with my machine. It doesn't work.

Teacher : Have you turned it on?

Joey : Yes, I have.

Teacher : OK. Let me see. Well, it's broken. I'll get you a new one.

Joey : Thank you.

Translation 中譯照過來

老師：你們都看過操作指南了嗎？

喬伊：是的。但是我的機器好像出了點問題。它不能運作了。

老師：你打開開關了嗎？

喬伊：是的，打開了。

老師：好的。讓我看看。嗯，是壞了。我去給你拿一台新的。

喬伊：謝謝您。

Key words 重點單字快速記

laboratory [ˋlæbrə͵torɪ] 名. 實驗室
instruction [ɪnˋstrʌkʃən] 名. 用法說明（複數）；操作指南
machine [məˋʃin] 名. 機器
work [wɝk] 動. 運轉
broken [ˋbrokən] 形. 壞的，不能使用的

Patterns 延伸句型快速學

01 *Have / Has + S + p.p. + ...?*

（某人已經……了嗎？）

Have you killed that cockroach?
你已經殺掉那隻蟑螂了嗎？

02 *It seems that ....*

（好像……。）

It seems that we cannot watch the meteor shower because of the thick cloud.
因為雲層厚，今天我們好像不能看到流星雨了。

Common Sense 小常識

超酷炫的美國大學實驗室

大學名稱	實驗室	相關職業	實驗內容
密蘇里科技大學	實驗煤礦	工業拆除	完美地爆破
喬治華盛頓大學	國家碰撞分析中心	安全工程師	把時速約 96km/h 的轎車撞向路邊設施
阿拉巴馬大學亨茨維爾分校	推進研究中心	火箭科學家	讓火箭飛得又快又遠
北肯塔基州大學	巴頓實驗室	地質學家	在地球上研究火星的生存條件
馬里蘭大學	太空系統實驗室	宇航服設計師	在零重力環境中測試新型宇航服
科羅拉多州立大學	發動機和能量轉換實驗室	機械工程師	製造一台更有力和更清潔的 2,300 馬力發動機
德州理工大學	風科學與工程研究中心	大氣科學家	將木板猛擊到牆上以衡量颶風的破壞
康乃爾大學	遊戲設計創意實驗室	視頻遊戲設計師	自己開發遊戲
加州大學美熹德	道森實驗室	海洋生物學家	與水母共潛
卡耐基梅隆大學	機器人研究所	機器人設計師	建構自動的多功能運動型車（SUV）

Key Sentences 基本句大變身

track075

1 I haven't read the instructions yet. 我還沒有看過操作指南。

- Have you gone through the instructions?
  你看過操作指南了嗎？
- I have read the instructions.
  我已經看過操作指南了。

2 You should get all the equipment ready. 你們應該把所有的設備都準備好。

- Are the equipment ready?
  設備準備好了嗎？
- Is the equipment in good condition?
  設備準備好了嗎？

3 There is a beaker on my desk. 我桌上有一個燒杯。

- There is no conical flask on my table.
  我的桌子上沒有錐形瓶。

4 The reagent is not for this experiment. 這個試劑不是這次實驗用的。

- Is the reagent here for the experiment?
  這種試劑是這次實驗用的嗎？
- Can I use this reagent for the experiment?
  我能用這種試劑做實驗嗎？

30 Examination 考試

Dialogue 1 第一次聊就上手

track076

Edward : It's time to study. Our chemistry exam is coming.

Bella : When is it?

Edward : July 15th.

Bella : What's on the test?

Edward : It seems to be from chapter three to chapter seven.

Bella : Well. I think I'm going to fail my chemistry exam.

Edward : Why are you so pessimistic?

Bella : I'm not being pessimistic. You know, my chemistry is so bad.

Edward : I believe you can pass the exam with good preparation. Don't lose your heart.

Bella : Thank you. That's very nice of you.

Translation 中譯照過來

愛德華：是時候念書了。我們的化學考試就要舉辦了。

貝　拉：什麼時候？

愛德華：7 月 15 號。

貝　拉：考哪些內容？

愛德華：好像是考第 3 章到第 7 章。

貝　拉：嗯。我覺得我的化學考試會不及格的。

愛德華：你為什麼這麼悲觀呢？

貝　拉：我這不是悲觀。你知道的，我的化學很不好。

愛德華：我相信你好好準備就會通過考試的。別灰心。

貝　拉：謝謝你。你真是太好了。

Key words 重點單字快速記

examination [ɪgˏzæməˋneʃən] 名. （尤指重要的）考試
chemistry [ˋkɛmɪstrɪ] 名. 化學
test [tɛst] 名. 測驗，測試；考查，考試
chapter [ˋtʃæptɚ] 名. 章節
fail [fel] 動. 不及格
pessimistic [ˏpɛsəˋmɪstɪk] 形. 悲觀的
pass [pæs] 動. （考試）及格；通過（考試）

Patterns 延伸句型快速學

01 ***It is time to V ....***
（該是時候……。）

It is time to go to bed.
該是上床睡覺的時候。

02 ***It seems to be ....***
（好像……。）

It seems to be too difficult for high school students.
這好像對中學生來說太困難了。

Common Sense 小常識

考試成績

美國的分數計算是以學分制，有 A, B, C, D 和 F 五個級別。F 表示不及格，學生需要重修得 F 的科目。因此美國學生分數差距沒有那麼明顯，考 100 分和考 90 分可能一樣都是 A。他們的最終成績既包含考試成績又包含作業成績，排名不公開。

Key Sentences 基本句大變身

track077

1	I've got a midterm the day after tomorrow.	我後天就要進行期中考試了。

- I've got a final exam this Friday.
  這週五我要進行期末考試。

2	What's on the test?	考哪些內容？

- What would we review for the test?
  這次考試我們要複習哪些內容？
- What the test will cover?
  考試會包含哪些內容？

3	I have to study.	我不得不念書了。

- It's time to read the books.
  是時候該看書了。
- We all have to cram.
  我們都得臨時抱佛腳。

4	I didn't pass the exam.	我沒通過考試。

- I failed in the exam.
  我考試沒及格。
- I have to take a make-up in math.
  我的數學必須得補考。

31 Studying Abroad 出國留學

Dialogue 1 第一次聊就上手

track078

Lisa : Hi, Jim. I want to study in a foreign country. Do you know what should I do first?

Jim : Yes. First, you should get application forms from some schools.

Lisa : How?

Jim : Write letters, make telephone calls or send E-mails to them.

Lisa : Will these do?

Jim : Yes. You have to contact ten to twelve schools.

Lisa : So I can receive ten to twelve application forms, right?

Jim : No. Only some will send you the application forms. The others might reject you.

Lisa : Got it.

Translation 中譯照過來

麗莎：嗨，吉姆。我想到國外留學。你知道首先應該怎麼做嗎？

吉姆：是的。首先，你應該向一些院校索取申請表。

麗莎：怎麼索取？

吉姆：向他們寫信、打電話或者發送電子郵件。

麗莎：用這些方法就可以了嗎？

吉姆：是的。你需要與 10 到 12 所院校聯繫。

麗莎：所以我就能得到 10 到 12 所院校寄來的申請表了，是嗎？

吉姆：不是那麼回事。只有部分院校會給你寄來申請表，剩下的可能會拒絕你。

麗莎：我懂了。

Key words 重點單字快速記

abroad [əˋbrɔd] 副 到國外，在國外
foreign [ˋfɔrɪn] 形 外國的
application [ˏæpləˋkeʃən] 名 申請（書）
form [fɔrm] 名 表格
contact [ˋkɑntækt] 動（寫信，打電話）聯繫（某人）
receive [rɪˋsiv] 動 收到
reject [rɪˋdʒɛkt] 動 不錄取；不雇用

Patterns 延伸句型快速學

01 ***S + have / has / had to + V + ...***
（某人必須……。）

> Nancy has to pick up her little brother.
> 南西必須去接她的弟弟。

02 ***Some .... The others ....***
（部分的……。剩下的……。）

> Some professors will not attend the workshop. The others will remain coming.
> 部分教授不會參加工作坊，剩下的仍會參加。

Common Sense 小常識

美國學生的作業

很多亞洲學生羨慕美國學生，認為美國學生大部分時間都在玩樂，基本沒有什麼作業，但事實並非如此。

美國老師也是會給學生留作業的，只是他們的作業不像亞洲國家一樣，單純鍛鍊孩子的重複力和背誦力。為了使學生更具思維力和靈活性，因此作業內容十分新穎，與現實生活也很接近。這些作業不但不會給學生帶來壓力，反而給他們的課外生活帶來了樂趣，讓他們將所學知識運用到實際生活中，對知識也能有更深層次的理解。

Key Sentences 基本句大變身

track079

1	I have no idea which country I want to go to.	我不知道我想去哪個國家。

- I don't know which country I should go to.
  我不知道我該去哪個國家。

2	Do I need to take any tests?	我需要參加什麼考試嗎？

- Do I have to take GRE?
  我必須得參加 GRE 考試嗎？
- Do you need to take an examination to go to graduate school?
  你讀研究生需要參加考試嗎？

3	What about the tuition there?	那裡的學費怎麼樣？

- Can I afford the tuition?
  我負擔得起學費嗎？
- Is the money sufficient to cover the tuition?
  這筆錢付學費夠嗎？

4	What's the difference between TOEFL and IELTS?	托福考試和雅思考試有什麼區別嗎？

- Do you intend to take the TOEFL test this year?
  你打算參加今年的托福考試嗎？
- The IELTS test is more difficult than other English tests.
  雅思考試比其他英語語言考試更難。

KNESS—A T IN
D FOR THE BEDSIDE LAMP AND TURNED IT
UINTING AT HIS SURROU
S, AND A COLOSSAL MAHOGANY FO
ILIAR RING. PI
ROOM WITH LOUIS XVI FURE, HAND-FRE S
SCOUR-POSTER BED.LA
HONE WAS RINGING IN THE A
D FOR THE BEDSIDE LAMP AND TURNED IT
UINTING AT HIS SURROU
S, AND A COLOSSAL MAHOGANY FO
ROOM WITH LOUIS XVI FURE, HAND-FRE S
SCOUR-POSTER BED.LA
IDE TABLE.TH
ON A CRUMPLED FLYER ON
UDLY PRESENTSA
DON PROFESSOR O
Y. A VISITOR? HIS EYES FOC
BCAN UNIVERSITY OF
RIN EVENING
GIOUS SYMBOLOGY, HARV
NIVERSITY LANGDO

Chapter 6

Work
工作篇

32 Applying for a Job 申請工作

Dialogue 1 第一次聊就上手

track080

Personnel : Good morning. This is ABC Company.

Chandler : Good morning. I'm calling about the job of editor.

Personnel : Well, the editor position is still opening.

Chandler : What are the requirements to apply for the editor?

Personnel : To do this job, you must have a degree in English.

Chandler : I see. If I want to apply for this position, what should I do?

Personnel : You can send your resume first, and I will inform you of the interview time.

Chandler : OK. Thank you very much.

Translation 中譯照過來

人事部：早安。這裡是 ABC 公司。

錢德勒：早安。我打電話是想瞭解一下編輯的職位。

人事部：嗯，編輯的職位目前還是空缺的。

錢德勒：應聘編輯這個職位的要求是什麼？

人事部：從事這個工作你必須具有英語專業的大學學位。

錢德勒：我知道了。如果我想應聘這個職位，我應該怎麼做呢？

人事部：你可以先發送你的簡歷，然後我會通知你面試的時間。

錢德勒：好的。非常感謝。

Key words 重點單字快速記

apply [əˋplaɪ] 動. 申請

requirement [rɪˋkwaɪrmənt]

名.（大學、雇主等的）要求，條件

editor [ˋɛdɪtɚ] 名. 編輯；編者

position [pəˋzɪʃən] 名. 職位，職務

resume [rɪˋzjum] 名. 個人簡歷

interview [ˋɪntɚˏvju] 名.（求職、入學等的）面試，面談

Patterns 延伸句型快速學

01 *To + V + O, S + V + O.*

（為了……，某人……。）

> To accomplish this mission, the special ops need to go stealth.
>
> 為了完成任務，特種部隊需要潛行。

02 *...inform sb of sth....*

（……通知某人某事。）

> We will inform every member of the new policy.
>
> 我們將通知所有會員新的政策。

Common Sense 小常識

美國人最怕的職業

在美國，有些工作不管工資有多高，也沒有太多人願意去嘗試。下面我們一起來看一看美國人不太喜歡的職業種類及其從業人數和報酬吧！

職業	人數（約）	平均小時工資（美元）
政治家	56,857	地方州：14.77 參議院和眾議院議員：174,000（年薪）
微生物學家	20,800	33.27
保全	1,163,023	11.88
犯罪現場偵查員	128,432	36.32
馴獸師	32,360	12.24
殯儀業者	27,505	23.13
無線電、蜂窩設備和信號樓設備安裝維修人員	16,213	21.97
單人脫口秀演員	37,272	16.89

Key 基本句大變身 Sentences

track081

1	What kinds of vacancies do you have?	你們有哪些職位空缺？

- What kinds of openings are available?
  現在有哪些職位空缺？
- Are there any vacancies?
  有職位空缺嗎？

2	I want to apply for the position of editor.	我想應聘編輯的職務。

- I'm coming for your advertisement for an editor.
  我是來應聘編輯的。
- I'd like to apply for the secretary position.
  我想應聘祕書的職位。

3	I'm calling about the job of editor.	我打電話是想了解一下編輯這個職位的情況。

- I'm inquiring about the job of editor.
  我想問一下有關編輯這個職位的情況。

4	What are the requirements to apply for the editor?	應聘編輯的要求是什麼？

- I'd like to know the requirements to apply for an editor.
  我想知道應聘一名編輯的要求是什麼。
- What do you think are the requirements for this post?
  你認為這個職位的要求是什麼？

33 Interview 面試

Dialogue 1 第一次聊就上手

track082

Interviewee : Good morning. My name's Jim Green.
Interviewer : Good morning, Mr. Green. Nice to meet you. Please sit down.
Interviewee : Thank you very much.
Interviewer : Can you show me your curriculum vitae?
Interviewee : Yes. Here you are.
Interviewer : OK. Do you have any working experiences?
Interviewee : I don't have any experiences as an editor, but I am diligent and I learn very fast.
Interviewer : OK. Can you make yourself easily understood in English?
Interviewee : Yes, in most circumstances.
Interviewer : What do you think of business travel?
Interviewee : I am young, and unmarried. So it's no problem for me to travel.
Interviewer : OK. That's all. I'll inform you if you get picked for next test.
Interviewee : Thank you very much.

Translation 中譯照過來

面試者：早上好。我叫吉姆 ・ 格林。
面試官：早上好，格林先生。很高興見到你。請坐。
面試者：非常感謝。
面試官：能讓我看看你的簡歷嗎？
面試者：好的，給您。
面試官：你有什麼工作經驗嗎？
面試者：我沒有任何編輯經驗，但是我非常勤奮，而且我學東西也非常快。
面試官：好的。你能毫無障礙的聽懂英文嗎？
面試者：是的，大部分時候都可以。
面試官：對於商務出差你是怎樣想的？
面試者：我年輕，而且還是單身。所以出差對我來説沒問題。
面試官：好的，面試完畢。如果你通過初試，我會通知你複試的。
面試者：非常感謝。

Key words 重點單字快速記

curriculum [kəˋrɪkjələm] 名. 課程

experience [ɪkˋspɪrɪəns] 名. 經驗；實踐

diligent [ˋdɪlədʒənt] 形. 勤奮的，勤勉的

circumstance [ˋsɝkəmˏstæns]
名. 情況（多用複數），情形

unmarried [ʌnˋmærɪd] 形. 未婚的；獨身的

Patterns 延伸句型快速學

01 *...as + N.*

（擔任……。）

Jason has a 5-year experience as a journalist.
傑森有五年擔任記者的經驗。

02 *It's no problem for sb to ....*

（對某人而言，……沒有問題。）

It's no problem for the squad to perform perfectly every time.
對隊伍來說，每次都完美演出是沒有問題的。

Common Sense 小常識

在美國面試，這些問題不用答（1）

在美國找工作面試時，有些問題面試官是不可以隨便詢問的，有的甚至是違法的。那麼面試者可以拒絕回答面試官的哪些問題呢？

＊你幾歲了？
＊你住在附近嗎？
＊你結婚了嗎？
＊你有孩子嗎？
＊你最初來自哪個國家？

待續……

33 Interview 面試

Dialogue 2 第一次聊就上手

track083

Interviewer : What are your weaknesses and strengths?

Interviewee : To be honest, I'm a poor speaker, but I'm studying how to speak in public now. My strength is that I can learn things very quickly.

Interviewer : If you are hired, what section would you like to work in?

Interviewee : If it is possible, I'd like to work in Marketing Department.

Interviewer : Do you have a driver's license?

Interviewee : Yes. And I have five years driving experience.

Interviewer : OK, that's good. I'll inform you the result as soon as possible. Goodbye.

Interviewee : OK. Goodbye.

Translation 中譯照過來

面試官：你的弱點和優點是什麼？

面試者：老實說，我不太擅長說話，但我正在學習如何在公眾場合說話。我的優點是我學東西很快。

面試官：如果被錄用了，你想在哪個部門工作？

面試者：如果可能的話，我想在銷售部工作。

面試官：你有駕照嗎？

面試者：有，而且我已經有 5 年的駕駛經驗了。

面試官：好的，很好。我會盡快通知你結果的。再見。

面試者：好的。再見。

Key words 重點單字快速記

weakness [ˋwiknɪs] 名. 缺點，不足
strength [strɛŋθ] 名. 優點，長處
hire [haɪr] 動. 雇用，聘任
section [ˋsɛkʃən] 名. 部門
license [ˋlaɪsn̩s] 名. 證照

Patterns 延伸句型快速學

01 *To be honest, ...*

（老實說，……。）

To be honest, I think my supervisor is overpaid.
老實說，我覺得我的主管薪水太高了。

02 *If it is possible, S + would like to + ...*

（如果可能的話，某人想……。）

If it is possible, I would like to go shopping tonight.
如果可能的話，我今晚想去購物。

Common Sense 小常識

在美國面試，這些問題不用答（2）

前述已提到一些面試者可以拒絕回答面試官的問題，讓我們多看一些：

＊你的宗教信仰是什麼？
＊你是否有欠款未還？
＊你被逮捕過嗎？
＊你最後一次使用禁藥是什麼時候？
＊你喜歡飲酒嗎？

Key Sentences 基本句大變身

track084

1	Where will the interview be?	面試在哪裡進行？

- When shall I have the interview?
  什麼時候給我面試？
- How long will the interview take?
  面試將持續多久？

2	I can stay focused in stressful situations.	我有面對困境的能力。

- I can handle changes flexibly.
  我可以靈活應對突發事件。
- I can communicate with all kinds of people.
  我可以和各種各樣的人溝通交往。

3	I have worked in DEF Company for three years.	我在 DEF 公司工作了三年。

- I have three years' experience in DEF Company.
  我在 DEF 公司有 3 年的工作經驗。

4	Salary isn't the only thing that is important to me.	薪水對我來說並不是唯一重要的事。

- Money is not the most important thing.
  錢並不是最重要的。

34 Hiring 錄用

Dialogue 1 第一次聊就上手

track085

Interviewer : What is your salary before?

Interviewee : Three thousand yuan per month.

Interviewer : What is your salary expectation now?

Interviewee : Five thousand yuan per month.

Interviewer : That's a little more than we had planned.

Interviewee : You'll find I'm worth it.

Translation 中譯照過來

面試官：你之前的薪水是多少？

面試者：每個月 3,000 元。

面試官：你現在所期望的薪水是多少呢？

面試者：每個月 5,000 元。

面試官：這比我們原來所計畫的多一些。

面試者：你們會發現我是值得拿那份薪水的。

Key words 重點單字快速記

salary [ˋsælərɪ] 名. 薪水
per [pɚ] 介. 每
expectation [͵ɛkspɛkˋteʃən] 名. 預料，預期
plan [plæn] 名. 計畫
worth [wɜθ] 名. 價值

Patterns 延伸句型快速學

01 *...than S had planned.*
（比原先計劃來的……。）

The distance of this route is much further than we had planned.
這條路的距離比我們預計的還要遠。

02 *S will find (that) ....*
（某人會發覺……。）

Sean will find that his girlfriend is cheating on him.
尚恩會發現他的女朋友正在他背後偷吃。

Common Sense 小常識

美國最好找工作的專業（1）

一提起熱門專業，大家首先想到的是金融、會計等好找工作的專業，但美國就業指導資訊網站卻列出了美國 10 大冷門但卻容易找到工作的專業：

1. 家庭和消費者學（Family and consumer sciences）
2. 語言學（Linguistics）
3. 娛樂管理（Recreation management）
4. 食品科學（Food science）
5. 包裝學（Packaging）

待續……

34 Hiring 錄用

Dialogue 2 第一次聊就上手

track086

Interviewee: Thank you for the interview yesterday.

Interviewer: You are welcome. What do you want to know about our company?

Interviewee: What do you think of the atmosphere here?

Interviewer: Frankly speaking, it's full of pressure. Can you handle it?

Interviewee: I really like that. It will make me full of energy.

Interviewer: I feel glad to hear that.

Translation 中譯照過來

面試者：感謝您昨天對我的面試。

面試官：不用客氣。對於我們公司你想了解什麼？

面試者：您覺得這裡的氛圍是怎樣的？

面試官：説實話，充滿了壓力，你能承受住嗎？

面試者：我真的喜歡這樣。它能讓我充滿了能量。

面試官：聽你這麼説我很高興。

Key words 重點單字快速記

company [ˋkʌmpənɪ] 名 公司
atmosphere [ˋætməsˏfɪr] 名 氣氛，環境
pressure [ˋprɛʃɚ] 名 （工作／生活中的）壓力
energy [ˋɛnɚdʒɪ] 名 力量，活力
glad [glæd] 形 高興的

Patterns 延伸句型快速學

01 *Frankly speaking, ...*

（說實話，……。）

Frankly speaking, the new system runs pretty slow.
說實話，新系統的作業速度頗慢。

02 *Sb / sth + will make + O + adj..*

（某人／某事使某人變得……。）

The upcoming movie will make me hot blooded.
接下來要上映的電影使我感到熱血沸騰。

Common Sense 小常識

美國最好找工作的專業（2）

前面提過，美國就業指導資訊網站列出了美國 10 大冷門但卻容易找到工作的專業，並已看過前 5 名，現在接著再看看其他的：

6. 犯罪學（Criminology）
7. 社會工作（Social work）
8. 城市研究（Urban studies）
9. 自然資源（Natural resources）
10. 老年學（Gerontology）

Key Sentences 基本句大變身

track087

1	What's your salary expectation?	你所期望的薪水是多少？

■ What's your expected salary?
你所期望的薪水是多少？

2	How long is my probation?	我的試用期是多長時間？

■ How long is the probation period?
試用期多長時間？

■ The first three months are probation period.
最初的三個月是試用期。

3	I expect to be paid according to my abilities.	我希望能根據我的能力支付薪資。

■ I hope to be paid according to my abilities.
我希望能根據我的能力支付薪資。

■ I want to be paid according to my abilities.
我希望能根據我的能力支付薪資。

4	With my experience, I'd like a salary of 3,000 dollars per month.	以我的經驗，我想要一個月3,000 美元的薪水。

■ Because of my experience, I'd like a salary of 3,000 dollars per month.
由於我有經驗，我想要一個月 3,000 美元的薪水。

■ Based on my experience, I'd like a salary of 3,000 dollars per month.
根據我的經驗，我想要一個月 3,000 美元的薪水。

35 Getting Familiar with New Job 熟悉新工作

Dialogue 1 第一次聊就上手

track088

Mary : Is this your first day to work here?

Kevin : Yes, I'm reporting for work today.

Mary : How do you feel?

Kevin : A little nervous.

Mary : Oh, please relax. Welcome to be one of us.

Kevin : Thank you.

Translation 中譯照過來

瑪麗：你是第一天來上班嗎？

凱文：是的，我今天來報到。

瑪麗：感覺如何啊？

凱文：有點緊張。

瑪麗：噢，請放鬆。歡迎你成為我們的一員。

凱文：謝謝。

Chapter1 交際篇
Chapter2 交通運輸篇
Chapter3 用餐事宜篇
Chapter4 愛情篇
Chapter5 校園生活篇
Chapter6 工作篇
Chapter7 購物篇
Chapter8 公共服務篇
Chapter9 情緒篇

Key words 重點單字快速記

familiar [fəˋmɪljɚ] 形. 熟悉的
report [rɪˋport] 動. 報到
feel [fil] 動. 感覺
nervous [ˋnɝvəs] 形. 緊張的
relax [rɪˋlæks] 動. 放心，鎮定

Patterns 延伸句型快速學

01 *Is this your first day to V ...?*

（這是你第一天……嗎？）

Is this your first day to New Zealand?
這是你第一天到紐西蘭嗎？

02 *Welcome (you) to ....*

（歡迎（你）……。）

Welcome to join our team.
歡迎加入我們團隊。

Common Sense 小常識

美國最有意義的工作（1）

在美國全國近 500 項工作中，超過百分之九十的人都認為下面的這些工作更具有人生意義，滿意度也更高：

職業	收入中位數（美元）
牧師	46,600
高校英語及文學教師	43,600
外科醫生	304,000
宗教活動及教育指導員	37,600
小學初中的學校管理人員	76,700
放射治療師	70,200

35 Getting Familiar with New Job 熟悉新工作

Dialogue 2 第一次聊就上手

track089

Smith: Welcome to our company!

Kevin: Thank you. I'm so happy to work here, Mr. Smith. Nice to meet you.

Smith: Nice to meet you, too. Now let me show you your office.

Kevin: After you.

Smith: Here is our office block. Your office is on the third floor. Please follow me.

Kevin: OK.

Translation 中譯照過來

史密斯：歡迎來到我們公司！

凱　文：謝謝。我很高興能來這裡上班，史密斯先生。很高興見到您。

史密斯：見到你我也很高興。現在我帶你去你的辦公室。

凱　文：請您帶路。

史密斯：這裡是我們的辦公大樓，你的辦公室在三樓。請跟我來。

凱　文：好的。

Key words 重點單字快速記

show [ʃo] 動. 展示；帶領
office [ˋɔfɪs] 名. 辦公室
block [blɑk] 名. 棟，座，幢
floor [flor] 名. 樓梯、樓層
follow [ˋfɑlo] 動. 跟隨

Patterns 延伸句型快速學

01 *Let me V ....*
（讓我做……。）

Let me bring you a hot towel.
讓我帶條新的熱毛巾給您。

02 *Here + is / are + N.*
（這裡是……。）

Here is the cafeteria of our company.
這是本公司的自助餐廳。

Common Sense 小常識

美國最有意義的工作（2）

剛剛已經看過了一些美國人普遍認為富有意義的工作，現在讓我們再來看一些：

職業	收入中位數（美元）
按摩師	60,100
精神醫生	197,000
麻醉師	273,000
康復輔導員	39,100
職業治療師	64,400
幼稚園教師	39,000
流行病學家	69,000

Key Sentences 基本句大變身

track090

1 Here is your job description. 這是你的職責說明。

- Please look at your job description.
  請看一下你的職責説明。
- Your main responsibility is seeing that the guest is safe.
  你的主要職責是確保客人的安全。

2 This is orientation week for all the new staff. 這是讓全體新員工熟悉情況的一週。

- Mr. Bush will introduce you to the details of your work.
  布希先生會使你熟悉工作的各項細節。

3 I'm glad you can join our team. 很高興你能加入我們的團隊。

- You are welcome to join us.
  我們非常樂意邀請你加入我們。
- We're very happy to have you. Welcome aboard.
  我們很高興你加入。歡迎加入我們的隊伍。

4 As a beginner, everything is very new to me. 作為一個新來的，一切對我來說都很生疏。

- I am still new to the work.
  我對這工作還不熟悉。
- I'm unfamiliar with the job.
  我對這工作還不熟悉。
- You'll get the feel of the work after you have been there a few weeks.
  你上班幾週後就會熟悉工作。

36 Getting Along with Co-workers 與同事相處

Dialogue 1 第一次聊就上手

track091

Lisa : Hey, Jack. Do you know the man over there?

Jack : The one with black hair or yellow hair?

Lisa : Yellow hair.
Jack : That's Mr. Green.
Lisa : Oh, I know him.
Jack : What do you think of him?
Lisa : I heard from my colleagues that he is a good manager.
Jack : That's a matter of opinion.
Lisa : What do you mean?
Jack : I worked with him for three years. That was the worst time in my career.

Translation 中譯照過來

麗莎：嘿，傑克。你認識那邊的那個人嗎？
傑克：黑頭髮的人還是黃頭髮的人？
麗莎：黃頭髮的。
傑克：那是格林先生。
麗莎：哦，我聽說過他。
傑克：你覺得他人怎麼樣？
麗莎：我聽同事說他是位好經理。
傑克：個人意見不同。
麗莎：此話怎講？
傑克：我跟他一起工作了三年。那是我職業生涯中最糟糕的時期。

Key words 重點單字快速記

coworker [ˋkoˏwɝkɚ] 名. 同事，同僚
colleague [ˋkɑlig] 名. 同事，同僚
manager [ˋmænɪdʒɚ] 名. 經理
opinion [əˋpɪnjən] 名. 意見
career [kəˋrɪr] 名. 職業，事業

Patterns 延伸句型快速學

01 *The one with + N.*

（那個有著……（特徵）的人。）

> The one with the long hair is the lead guitar of the band.
> 那個有著長髮的人是這個樂團的首席吉他手。

02 *I heard from sb that ....*

（我聽某人說……。）

> I heard from Hanson that our budget is getting a cut.
> 我聽漢森說，我們的預算被刪減了。

Common Sense 小常識

認清工作時的客套話

在職業生涯中，"I can help you."（我能幫助您。）是每個美國人經常聽到的一句話。眾所周知，美國人的合作精神是一流的，與此同時，他們的客套也是一流的。"I can help you." 這句話在美國人口中與我們的「您吃飯了嗎？」其實沒什麼區別，並不意味著他們當真會來幫助你。因此，如果初次與美國人接觸，不要輕信了這句話，否則肯定會大失所望。

Key Sentences 基本句大變身

track092

1	He gets along well with his co-workers.	他跟同事很合得來。

- He gets on well with Jack.
  他與傑克很合得來。
- He doesn't get along well with her.
  他跟她合不來。

2	I respect her.	我很尊敬她。

- I look up to her.
  我很尊敬她。
- I despise her.
  我瞧不起她。
- I look down on her.
  我瞧不起她。

3	She didn't pay any attention to me at all.	她根本就不關注我。

- She always ignores me.
  她總是忽視我。
- She always gives me the cold shoulder.
  她總是對我很冷漠。

4	He is a brownnoser.	他是個馬屁精。

- He is a real apple polisher.
  他真是個馬屁精。
- I don't like the man who licks his leader's boots.
  我不喜歡拍主管馬屁的人。

37 Working Overtime 加班

Dialogue 1 第一次聊就上手

track093

Kevin : It's dark outside.

Mary : Yes. It's time to go home.

Kevin : But I have to work overtime tonight.

Mary : Wow, you work so hard.

Kevin : The report is getting down to the wire.

Mary : Poor Kevin.

Translation 中譯照過來

凱文：外面天都黑了。

瑪麗：是啊，該回家了。

凱文：但是今晚我得加班了。

瑪麗：哇，你工作真努力啊。

凱文：這個報告期限就快到了。

瑪麗：可憐的凱文。

Chapter1 交際篇
Chapter2 交通運輸篇
Chapter3 用餐事宜篇
Chapter4 愛情篇
Chapter5 校園生活篇
Chapter6 工作篇
Chapter7 購物篇
Chapter8 公共服務篇
Chapter9 情緒篇

Key words 重點單字快速記

dark [dɑrk] 形. 黑暗的
overtime [ˌovɚˋtaɪm] 副. 加班地
hard [hɑrd] 形. 辛苦的
report [rɪˋport] 名. 報告
wire [waɪr] 名. 金屬絲

Patterns 延伸句型快速學

01 ***S + V + so adv. ....***
（某人（做某事）非常……。）

> That girl studies so hard for the exam.
> 那女孩為了考試而學習地非常認真。

02 ***... down to the wire.***
（直到最後一刻……。）

> The application date of the sponsorship is getting down to the wire.
> 獎助金的申請期限就快要到了。

Common Sense 小常識

美國人的工作和休息

美國人工作和休息時間分明，時間點一到，該做什麼就做什麼，不能互相干擾。通常情況下，他們和工作相關的事務都會在工作時間完成，在談判桌上就會拍板達成一致的共識。

37 Working Overtime 加班

Dialogue 2 第一次聊就上手

track094

Tyler : I have a bad news for you.

Sophie : What is it?

Tyler : We have to work overtime tonight.

Sophie : Oh, I hate that.

Tyler : Me too. It goes against my plan.

Sophie : Yeah. I have to rearrange my schedule, too.

Tyler : We don't have other options, do we?

Sophie : OK. What's the plan in detail?

Tyler : We have to work three more hours tonight and tomorrow night.

Translation 中譯照過來

泰勒：我有一個壞消息要告訴你。

索菲：什麼壞消息？

泰勒：今晚我們得加班了。

索菲：噢，我討厭加班。

泰勒：我也是，違背了我的計畫。

索菲：是啊。我也得重新安排我的日程。

泰勒：我們別無選擇了，對吧？

索菲：好吧。具體的加班計畫是什麼呢？

泰勒：今晚和明晚我們要多上 3 個小時的班。

Key words 重點單字快速記

hate [het] 動. 討厭

rearrange [ˌriəˋrendʒ] 動. 重新安排（會期等）

schedule [ˋskɛdʒul] 名. 行程

option [ˋɑpʃən] 名. 選擇；可選擇的東西

detail [ˋditel] 名. 細節

Patterns 延伸句型快速學

01 *Sth goes against + N.*

（某事違背了……。）

What his stepmother doing goes against his father's will.

他繼母所做所為與他父親的遺囑相違背。

02 *S + V + O, too.*

（某人也……。）

He tries to win that English competition, too.

他也嘗試想在那個英語競賽中獲勝。

Common Sense 小常識

美國人的工作和休息

每週五晚上通常是美國人與朋友相聚的時間，他們在一起唱歌、跳舞、喝酒、聊天，玩得不亦樂乎。每週末則會與家人或幾個不錯的朋友開車出去玩。

Key 基本句大變身 Sentences

track095

1 Can you work overtime this week? 你這週能加班嗎？

- You'd better work overtime this week.
  你這週最好加個班。
- I will work overtime this week.
  這週我要加班。

2 We don't get paid for overtime. 我們沒有加班費。

- Do you get overtime pay?
  你有加班費嗎？
- They were paid extra for overtime.
  他們拿到了加班費。
- The over rate is one and a half times normal pay.
  加班費是正常工資的 1.5 倍。

3 I hate to say this, but I have to ask you to work overtime. 我討厭這樣說，但是我不得不請你加班。

- Though I don't want to, I have to ask you to work overtime.
  雖然我不想這樣，但我得請你加班。
- The boss said we were likely to work overtime today.
  老闆說我們今天很可能要加班。

38 Asking for a Leave 請假

Dialogue 1 第一次聊就上手

track096

Kevin : Excuse me, manager. Can I ask for a leave tomorrow?

Manager : Why?

Kevin : There are some personal affairs.

Manager : You'll be deducted for this.

Kevin : I know. That's OK.

Manager : Then who will do the work for you?

Kevin : I have already asked Jack to cover for me.

Manager : That's OK.

Translation 中譯照過來

凱文：打擾一下，經理。我明天可以請假嗎？

經理：為什麼？

凱文：有些個人事務。

經理：這樣會扣你工資的。

凱文：我知道，沒關係。

經理：那你的工作誰替你負責呢？

凱文：我已經請傑克幫我了。

經理：那好吧。

Key words 重點單字快速記

leave [liv] 名. 假期
personal [ˋpɝsn̩l] 形. 個人的，私人的
affair [əˋfɛr] 名. 個人的事，私事
deduct [dɪˋdʌkt] 動. 減去，扣除
cover [ˋkʌvɚ] 動. 代替（某人的工作）[+ for]

Patterns 延伸句型快速學

01 *Can I ask for + N?*

（我可以要求……嗎？）

> Can I ask for an extra donut?
> 我可以多要一個甜甜圈嗎？

02 *Sb / Sth will be deducted for ....*

（某人／某物將因為……被扣除。）

> Your scores will be deducted for the violation.
> 你的積分將因為違規而被扣除。

Common Sense 小常識

美國人的奇葩請假理由（1）

假眼球掉了。
在高速公路時假牙飛出窗外。
迷路了。
不知道穿什麼上班。
心情不好，怕上班傷到同事。

38 Asking for a Leave 請假

Dialogue 2 第一次聊就上手

track097

Monica : May I ask for leave, sir?

Manager : What's wrong with you?

Monica : My son is ill, and I have to take care of him.

Manager : I'm sorry to hear that. But you know we're so busy these days.

Monica : I know that, but no one can look after my son.

Manager : OK. I will find someone to cover for you.

Monica : Thank you very much.

Translation 中譯照過來

莫妮卡：我可以請假嗎，先生？

經　理：你怎麼了？

莫妮卡：我兒子病了，我得照顧他。

經　理：聽到這個消息我很抱歉。不過你也知道，我們現在很忙。

莫妮卡：我知道，但沒有人照顧我兒子。

經　理：好吧。我會找人代替你的。

莫妮卡：非常感謝您。

Key words 重點單字快速記

wrong [rɔŋ] 形. 出毛病的
ill [ɪl] 形. 生病的
sorry [ˋsɑrɪ] 形. 感到難過的
busy [ˋbɪzɪ] 形. 忙碌的
someone [ˋsʌm͵wʌn] 代. 某人

Patterns 延伸句型快速學

01 *I'm sorry to hear (that)....*
（我很抱歉聽到……。）

> I'm sorry to hear that your grandmother passed away.
> 我很抱歉聽到您的祖母過世了。

02 *A look after B.*
（A照顧B。）

> My friend James will look after my cat while I go abroad.
> 我朋友詹姆士會在我出國期間幫忙照顧我的貓。

Common Sense 小常識

美國人的奇葩請假理由（2）

車被蜜蜂包圍了。
最喜歡的橄欖球隊輸了比賽，很痛心，需要療傷。
咬到舌頭了。
不知道誰把我們家門窗封住了，沒辦法出門。
戒煙呢，心情不好。

Key Sentences 基本句大變身

track098

1	Would you mind if I come in at 9:30 tomorrow?	如果我明天九點半來上班，您不會介意吧？

- Would you mind my coming late at 9:30 tomorrow?
  你介意我明天晚點到九點半再來嗎？

2	I want to ask a few days off.	我想請幾天假。

- Can I have one day off?
  我能請一天假嗎？
- Can I have Tuesday afternoon off to see my doctor?
  我能在週二下午請假去看病嗎？

3	I'm afraid I can't come to work today.	恐怕今天我不能來上班了。

- I'm sorry that I can't come to work today.
  抱歉，今天我不能來上班了。
- I can't make it to work today. I've got the flu.
  我今天不能去上班了。我得了流感。

4	When will you be back?	你什麼時候回來？

- I will be back to work after I recover.
  我痊癒後就回去上班。
- I will be back in three days.
  我三天後回去。

39 Being Late for Work 遲到

Dialogue 1 第一次聊就上手

track099

Lucy : Sorry, I overslept. My alarm didn't go off this morning.

Manager : Again?

Lucy : Yes. That's the truth.

Manager : Your clock never works. I think you need to buy a new one.

Lucy : Well, maybe.

Translation 中譯照過來

露西：對不起，我睡過頭了。我的鬧鐘今早沒有響。

經理：又沒響？

露西：是的，是真的。

經理：你的鬧鐘從來就沒有正常工作過。我想你該買個新的了。

露西：嗯，可能吧。

Key words 重點單字快速記

late [let] 形. 晚的，遲到的
oversleep [ˋovəˋslip] 動. 睡得太久，睡過頭
alarm [əˋlɑrm] 名. 鬧鐘
truth [truθ] 名. 真相
clock [klɑk] 名. 鬧鐘

Patterns 延伸句型快速學

01 *Sth doesn't / didn't go off ....*

（某物沒有正常運作……。）

The SWAT team defused that bomb in time, so it didn't go off.
特警隊及時拆除了炸彈，所以炸彈並沒有爆炸。

02 *I think (that) ....*

（我想……。）

I think that you need to take a day off.
我覺得你該休假一天。

Common Sense 小常識

時間就是金錢

美國的工作者不管是上班還是參加會議都會準時出席，他們認為工作日不工作就是浪費金錢。美國人習慣按時間執行任務，崇尚單一事件文化。

39 Being Late for Work 遲到

Dialogue 2 第一次聊就上手

track100

Phoebe : Sorry, I'm late.

Chandler : You have been late for three days.

Phoebe : Oh, really?

Chandler : Yes, you need to get here on time tomorrow.

Phoebe : I have insomnia these days.

Chandler : I can understand. But if our boss finds out, he will be angry.

Phoebe : I know. Thank you for reminding.

Translation 中譯照過來

菲　比：抱歉，我來晚了。

錢德勒：你已經遲到三天了。

菲　比：噢，真的嗎？

錢德勒：是的，你明天需要準時到這裡。

菲　比：我這幾天老失眠。

錢德勒：我能理解。但是，如果老闆發現的話，他會生氣的。

菲　比：我知道。謝謝你的提醒。

Chapter1 交際篇
Chapter2 交通運輸篇
Chapter3 用餐事宜篇
Chapter4 愛情篇
Chapter5 校園生活篇
Chapter6 工作篇
Chapter7 購物篇
Chapter8 公共服務篇
Chapter9 情緒篇

Key words 重點單字快速記

insomnia [ɪnˋsɑmnɪə] 名. 失眠
understand [ˏʌndɚˋstænd] 動. 理解
boss [bɔs] 名. 老闆
angry [ˋæŋgrɪ] 形. 生氣的
remind [rɪˋmaɪnd] 動. 提醒

Patterns 延伸句型快速學

01 ***S + have / has ... + for +*** 一段時間 .
（某人已經……（一段時間）了。）

The flood has struck the town for a week.
洪水已侵襲小鎮一週了。

02 ***If S + V, S + will + V.***
（如果某人……，某人將……。）

If I get a cheap ticket, I will fly to Japan immediately.
如果我買到便宜的機票，我會馬上飛去日本。

Common Sense 小常識

時間就是金錢

與美國人相處一定要堅守時間觀念，不要視之為「友情連結」，如遇緊急情況可能遲到，則一定要提前打電話告知。

Key Sentences 基本句大變身

track101

1 You need to be here on time. 你得準時到這裡。

- You need to arrive here punctually.
  你得準時到這裡。

2 My alarm didn't go off this morning. 我的鬧鐘今早沒有響。

- My alarm is broken.
  我的鬧鐘壞了。

3 Can't you take an early bus? 你不能坐早一班的車來嗎？

- Isn't it possible for you to take an early bus?
  你不能坐早班的車來嗎？
- Can't you leave home earlier?
  你不能早點從家裡出發嗎？

4 Now I'll call the roll. 現在我要點名了。

- The manager is calling the roll now.
  經理現在正在點名。
- Don't forget to punch your time card.
  別忘了打你的出勤卡。

40 Promotion & Pay Raise 升職加薪

Dialogue 1 第一次聊就上手

track102

Kevin : I heard that Lucy has been promoted as the sales manager.

Mary : Really?

Kevin : That's true. It has been announcement on the bulletin board.

Mary : That's great.

Kevin : Yes. I'm so glad for her.

Translation 中譯照過來

凱文：我聽說露西被擢升為銷售經理了。

瑪麗：真的嗎？

凱文：真的。布告欄上都宣布了。

瑪麗：那太好了。

凱文：是啊。我真替她感到高興。

Key words 重點單字快速記

promotion [prəˋmoʃən] 名. 提升，晉升

raise [rez] 名. 加薪

announcement [əˋnaʊnsmənt]

名.（重要／正式）通告，宣告

bulletin [ˋbʊlətɪn] 名. 公告；公報；告示

board [bord] 名. 佈告牌，公告牌

Patterns 延伸句型快速學

01 ***Sb + be promoted as + N.***

（某人被升職為……。）

> Cindy has been promoted as a chief executive officer.
>
> 辛蒂被升職為執行長了。

02 ***Sb + be + so glad for + sb / sth....***

（某人為某人／某事感到高興。）

> My parents are so glad for my brother for getting his bachelor's degree.
>
> 我父母為我弟弟取得學士學位感到高興。

Common Sense 小常識

如何加薪（1）

在美國，很多公司會採取凍結薪金或減少員工工資的方法來應對各種危機，且加薪都是以百分比的方式調整的，老員工起薪相對較低，因此在一個公司待得時間越長，工資反而越低。

那要如何加薪呢？後面我們會提到。

40 Promotion & Pay Raise 升職加薪

Dialogue 2 第一次聊就上手

track103

Boss : I'm satisfied with your achievement.

Lucy : I am flattered by your admiration.

Boss : I decided to promote you as manager.

Lucy : Thank you. I will work harder and not let you down.

Boss : I trust you.

Translation 中譯照過來

老闆：我對你的業績非常滿意。

露西：您的讚賞讓我受寵若驚。

老闆：我決定提拔你當經理。

露西：謝謝。我會更加努力工作，不會讓您失望的。

老闆：我相信你。

Key words 重點單字快速記

satisfied [`sætɪs͵faɪd] 形. 感到滿意
achievement [ə`tʃivmənt] 名. 成績；成就
admiration [͵ædmə`reʃən] 名. 敬佩，欽佩
decided [dɪ`saɪdɪd] 形. 決定了的
manager [`mænɪdʒɚ] 名. 經理

Patterns 延伸句型快速學

01 ***Sb + be satisified with + sth.***
（某人對某事感到滿意。）

> My supervisor is satisfied with my performance.
> 我主管對我的表現感到滿意。

02 ***Sb + be flattered by + sth.***
（某人對某事感到受寵若驚。）

> I am flattered by Lucy's recommendation.
> 我對露西的推薦感到受寵若驚。

Common Sense 小常識

如何加薪（2）

前面提過，因為在一間公司待的時間越長，基本薪資會越低，我們也就不難理解為什麼美國人會出現兩年一次的跳槽現象了。員工跳槽後不僅工資會有所增加，職位也會提升，但跳槽後心理壓力會增大，而且並不是所有人都具備跳槽的資質。

Key Sentences 基本句大變身

track104

1	I'm recommending you for promotion.	我要舉薦你升職。

- I will give you a promotion.
  我要給你升職。
- It's my considered opinion that you should be promoted.
  經過認真考慮，我認為你應該被升職。

2	Your aggressiveness impressed me a lot.	你的幹勁讓我印象深刻。

- Your achievement impressed me a lot.
  你的成績讓我印象深刻。
- You impressed me with your diligence.
  你的勤奮讓我印象深刻。
- I was quite impressed by your dogged determination to succeed.
  你想成功的堅定決心讓我印象深刻。

3	I'm satisfied with the raise.	這次加薪我很滿意。

- It is our practice to give annual raises.
  每年加薪是我們的慣例。
- He grasped the opportunity to ask for a higher salary.
  他抓住機會要求加薪。

4	Have you decided to give me a pay raise?	你決定給我加薪了嗎？

- Did you ask your boss for a raise?
  你向你的老闆要求加薪了嗎？
- You promised to give me a pay raise after probation.
  你答應過我試用期後給我加薪。

41 Getting the Sack 被解雇

Dialogue 1 第一次聊就上手

track105

Lucy : Hi, Jack. Why are you so upset?

Jack : I was fired yesterday.

Lucy : For what?

Jack : For being late for work.

Lucy : Well, that's your fault. I think you need to go to work on time when you get a new job.

Jack : I think so, too.

Translation 中譯照過來

露西：嗨，傑克。你為什麼這麼沮喪？

傑克：昨天我被解雇了。

露西：為什麼？

傑克：因為上班遲到。

露西：好吧，那就是你的錯了。我覺得你應該找到新工作後準時上班。

傑克：我也這樣認為。

Key words 重點單字快速記

sack [sæk] 名. 解僱　動. 解僱
upset [ʌpˋsɛt] 形. 心煩意亂的，煩惱的
fire [faɪr] 動. 開除，解雇
fault [fɔlt] 名. 責任，過錯
need [nid] 動. 需要

Patterns 延伸句型快速學

01 *...when....*

（當……時，……。）

Sandra has shown her potential when she first joined the team.
當珊卓加入隊伍時，她就展現了她的潛力。

02 *Sb + think so, too.*

（某人也這樣認為。）

Matt isn't qualified for this position. Even his supervisor thinks so, too.
麥特無法勝任這個職位，連他的主管也這麼認為。

Common Sense 小常識

美國 10 大鐵飯碗

1. 脊椎按摩師
2. 牙醫
3. 醫師助理
4. 內科和外科醫生
5. 農場、牧場和其他農業生產場所的管理者
6. 醫療、牙科和眼科實驗室技師
7. 偵探和刑事偵查員
8. 語言障礙矯正師
9. 郵政業郵遞員
10. 航太工程師

Key Sentences 基本句大變身

track106

1 You are fired. 你被解雇了。

- The manager dismissed him yesterday.
  昨天經理把他解雇了。
- He got the pink slip yesterday.
  他昨天收到了解雇通知書。

2 We have to lay off some staff. 我們不得不裁減一些員工。

- We have to fire some staff.
  我們不得不裁減一些員工。
- We have to dismiss some staff.
  我們不得不裁減一些員工。

3 He got the sack because of being late for work. 他因為總遲到而被解雇了。

- He was sacked because he was always late for work.
  他因為遲到而被解雇了。
- He was fired for slacking at work.
  他因為工作偷懶被解雇了。
- He was dismissed for neglecting his duty.
  他因為怠忽職守而被解雇了。

4 When he was dismissed? 他是什麼時候被解雇的？

- Why he was fired?
  他為什麼被解雇了？
- When were you let out from your job?
  你什麼時候被解雇的？

42 Applying for Resignation 辭職

Dialogue 1 第一次聊就上手

track107

Ada : I want to quit my current job.

Manager : Why?

Ada : Although I like my job, I haven't had any promotion these years.

Manager : I agree with you up to a point, but please think twice before you leap.

Translation 中譯照過來

艾達：我想辭掉現在的工作。

經理：為什麼？

艾達：雖然我喜歡我的工作，但是這些年我都沒有被升官過。

經理：在某些方面我同意你的想法，不過你還是要三思而後行。

Key words 重點單字快速記

resignation [ˌrɛzɪgˈneʃən] 名. 辭職；辭職信
quit [kwɪt] 動. 離開（工作崗位、學校等）
current [ˈkɝənt] 形. 現時的，當前的
point [pɔɪnt] 名. 思想；觀點
leap [lip] 動. 跳

Patterns 延伸句型快速學

01 *Although..., ...*
（雖然……，但是……。）

Although I am not so good at leather crafting, I made a lot of leather bags lately.
雖然我不太擅長皮作，但是我最近仍做了許多皮包。

02 *S + V + O + up to a point.*
（某種程度上，……。）

The method works up to a point, but not for all circumstances.
這個方法某種程度上行得通，但無法適用於所有情況。

Common Sense 小常識

美國人的奇葩辭職理由（1）

想要靠信託基金生活。
覺得自己錢賺得太多，不缺這份薪水。
早上怎麼也起不來。
不想穿西裝。
想在家裡餵狗。
想在工作時間陪女友看電影。

42 Applying for Resignation 辭職

Dialogue 2 第一次聊就上手

track108

Manager : Can I help you?

Joe : It's hard to say, but I've found a position at another company.

Manager : Why do you want to leave?

Joe : I think the job here doesn't suit me.

Manager : Well. That's fine. If there is anything I can do for you, please let me know.

Joe : Thank you very much.

Translation 中譯照過來

經理：我能幫你什麼嗎？

喬伊：這很難開口，但我已經在另一家公司找到了一份工作。

經理：你為什麼要離開呢？

喬伊：我覺得這裡的工作不適合我。

經理：好吧，沒關係。如果有需要我幫忙的，請儘管說。

喬伊：非常感謝。

Key words 重點單字快速記

position [pəˋzɪʃən] 名. 職位
another [əˋnʌðɚ] 代. 另一個
leave [liv] 動. 離開
job [dʒɑb] 名. 工作
suit [sut] 動. 適合

Patterns 延伸句型快速學

01 *It is / was adj. to V ....*

（做某個動作是……的。）

It is not right to judge other people by their appearance.
以貌取人是不對的。

02 *It there is ..., please ....*

（如果有……，請……。）

If there is any new product, please mail me the latest catalog.
如果有任何新產品，請寄給我最新的目錄。

Common Sense 小常識

美國人的奇葩辭職理由（2）

想要去種蘋果。
想要加入馬戲團。
想要參加選美比賽。
老闆弄丟了我送他的狗。
討厭公司的地毯。
想要去登珠穆朗瑪峰。

Key Sentences 基本句大變身

track109

1	I would like to quit my current job.	我想辭掉現在的工作。

■ I want to quit my current job.
我想辭掉現在的工作。

2	I think that I cannot grow anymore in this company.	我覺得在這個公司沒有成長空間了。

■ I sense that I cannot grow anymore in this company.
我覺得在這個公司沒有成長空間了。

3	I want to leave the company to seek for development.	我想離開公司另謀發展。

■ I need to seek for more development.
我需要尋求更多的發展。

4	I'm interested in positions in other companies.	別的公司有我感興趣的職位。

■ I've found a position in another company.
我已經在另一家公司找到了一份工作。

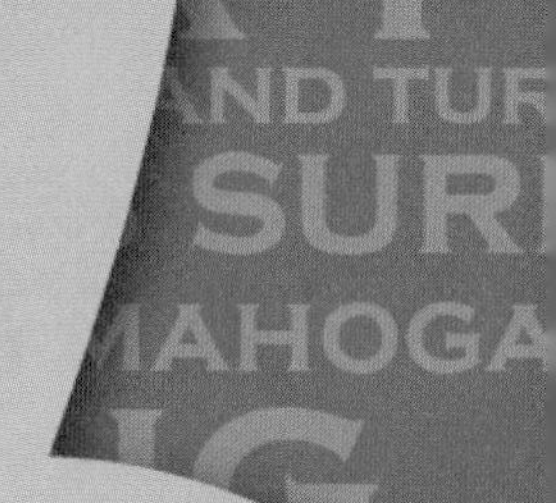

Chapter 7

Shopping
購物篇

43 At the Department Store 在百貨公司

Dialogue 1 第一次聊就上手

track110

Caroline : How about going shopping with me tomorrow?

Bonnie : Why not? I almost have no clothes to wear.

Caroline : Then how about going to the department store at 8 am?

Bonnie : Do we have to meet so early?

Caroline : Yes. Because it will be too crowded in the afternoon.

Translation 中譯照過來

卡洛琳：明天一起去逛街怎麼樣？

邦　妮：為什麼不呢？我幾乎沒有衣服穿了。

卡洛琳：那早上 8 點去百貨公司如何？

邦　妮：我們必須要那麼早去嗎？

卡洛琳：嗯，因為下午會很擁擠啊。

Key words 重點單字快速記

department store [dɪˋpɑrtmənt stor] 名. 百貨公司
shopping [ˋʃɑpɪŋ] 名. 購物
almost [ˋɔlˏmost] 副. 幾乎
clothes [kloz] 名. 衣服
crowded [ˋkraʊdɪd] 形. 擁擠的

Patterns 延伸句型快速學

01 ***Why not + Ving ...?***
（為什麼不……呢？）

Why not taking a photo of this beautiful scene?
為什麼不拍下這美麗的景色？

02 ***S + be + too + adj. + ...***
（太……。）

These pants are too tight for me.
這些長褲對我來說太緊了。

Common Sense 小常識

在美國購物（1）

美國的購物商城五花八門。除了沃爾瑪、梅西百貨、希爾斯百貨等大型賣場，還有像是 Safeway、Giant 等中型超市。

43 At the Department Store 在百貨公司

Dialogue 2 第一次聊就上手

track111

Salesclerk : Can I help you?

Bonnie : I am just browsing.

Salesclerk : Our clothes are all this year's new style!

Bonnie : Sorry, I don't need to buy clothes now.

Salesclerk : Just come in and have a look. They are all of fashion.

Bonnie : I said I was just looking around!

Translation 中譯照過來

售貨員：我能幫您嗎？

邦　妮：我只是隨便看看。

售貨員：我們的衣服都是今年的新款！

邦　妮：抱歉，我現在不需要買衣服。

售貨員：進來看看吧，它們都很時尚。

邦　妮：我說過了我只是隨便看看而已！

Key words 重點單字快速記

just [dʒʌst] 副. 只是
browse [brauz] 動.（在商店裡）隨便看看
style [staɪl] 名. 款式
look [lʊk] 動. 看看
fashion [ˋfæʃən] 名. 時尚；流行款式

Patterns 延伸句型快速學

01 ***I am just Ving.***
（我只是……。）

> I am just kidding.
> 我只是開玩笑罷了

02 ***I said (that) ....***
（我說過……。）

> I said that Nancy is the captain of the cheer leading squad.
> 我說過南西是啦啦隊隊長。

Common Sense 小常識

在美國購物（2）

美國也有很多中小型便民超市，它們的服務項目各具特色，有食品店、盥洗用品店和藥品店，同時也有雜貨店。現在，也有很多來自各國的商人在美國開設了具有異國特色的店鋪。

Key Sentences 基本句大變身

track112

1 I am just browsing. 我只是隨便看看。

- I just want to do some window-shopping.
  我只是看看。
- I just look around.
  我只是到處看看。

2 I want to buy something off-the-rack. 我只想隨便買幾件衣服。

- I just want to pick up some things for the children.
  我只想順便給孩子買點東西。

3 I haven't a penny to my name. 我身無分文。

- I'm on the rocks.
  我身無分文。
- I'm quite penniless.
  我身無分文。

4 When does the store close? 商店什麼時候關門？

- When is the closing time?
  什麼時候關門？

44 Clothes 服飾

Dialogue 1 第一次聊就上手

track113

Salesclerk : What can I do for you, madam?

Lisa : I'd like to buy a dress.

Salesclerk : What is your size?

Lisa : Medium should be fine.

Salesclerk : Is this one OK?

Lisa : May I try it on?

Salesclerk : Certainly. The fitting room is in the right corner.

(later)

Lisa : What do you think?

Salesclerk : It looks great on you.

Lisa : I would like to take it.

Translation 中譯照過來

售貨員：能為您做點什麼嗎，女士？

莉　薩：我需要買一件裙子。

售貨員：您穿什麼尺寸的？

莉　薩：中號的就可以。

售貨員：這件怎麼樣？

莉　薩：我能試穿嗎？

售貨員：當然可以。試衣間在右邊轉角。

（過了一會兒）

莉　薩：你覺得怎麼樣？

售貨員：您穿起來很好看。

莉　薩：我想要買下來。

Key words 重點單字快速記

madam [ˋmædəm] 名. 女士；夫人
dress [drɛs] 名. 洋裝
size [saɪz] 名. 尺碼，號
medium [ˋmidɪəm] 形. 中號的
fitting [ˋfɪtɪŋ] 形. 合適的
corner [ˋkɔrnɚ] 名. 轉角

Patterns 延伸句型快速學

01 *Sth should be fine.*
（某物應該可以。）

> A cup of coffee should be fine for me.
> 給我一杯咖啡應該就可以了。

02 *Sth looks adj. ....*
（某物看起來……。）

> That painting looks marvelous.
> 那幅畫看起來令人驚嘆。

Common Sense 小常識

根據臉型挑衣服（1）

人的臉型有橢圓形、圓形、倒三角形、正三角形、長形、方形、菱形七種，不同的臉型適合穿不同的衣服：

橢圓形臉：這種臉型俗稱鵝蛋臉，各種衣服都適合穿，如果選擇有特色一點的衣服更能顯示出個人的個性和氣質。

圓形臉：這種臉型也就是娃娃臉。這種臉型的人穿 V 字領或大翻領的衣服更好看。

待續……

Dialogue 2 第一次聊就上手

track114

David : Well, Lisa, what do you think?

Lisa : Mmm, it's nice, but I think you need a slightly smaller size.

David : I think this is the only one. I'd better ask an assistant. Excuse me? Do you have this in a size 12?

Salesclerk : I'm afraid everything in the sale is out on display.

David : Oh dear, it's just a bit too loose.

Salesclerk : I think we have a size 12 in yellow.

David : Oh no. Yellow's just not my color.

Salesclerk : It's not bright yellow. It's a nice dark yellow. Here it is. Why don't you try it on? There's a fitting room free over there.
(later)

David : It fits like a glove. What do you think Lisa?

Lisa : It looks really nice. I guess yellow suits you after all.

Translation 中譯照過來

戴維：那麼，莉莎，你覺得怎麼樣？

莉莎：嗯，很好，但我覺得你需要稍微小一號的。

戴維：我覺得只有這一件了。我最好問一下店員。打擾一下，這件衣服你們有尺寸 12 的嗎？

店員：恐怕所有待售的衣服都陳列在外面了。

戴維：哦，天哪，它有一點點寬鬆。

店員：我想我們有件黃色的是尺寸 12。

戴維：哦，不要。黃色不適合我。

店員：不是亮黃色的，它是一件很漂亮的深黃色的，拿去。您為什麼不試試呢？那邊有一個更衣室沒人。
（過了一會兒）

戴維：完全合適。莉莎你覺得怎麼樣？

莉莎：看起來真的很棒。黃色大概是最適合你的顏色了。

Key words 重點單字快速記

slightly [ˋslaɪtlɪ] 副. 略微，稍微
assistant [əˋsɪstənt] 名. 助理
sale [sel] 名. 出售，銷售
display [dɪˋsple] 名. 陳列，展示
loose [lus] 形. 寬大的，寬鬆的
glove [glʌv] 名. 手套

Patterns 延伸句型快速學

01 *I'm afraid (that) ....*
（我擔心……。）

I'm afraid that no one will survive that collision.
我擔心在那撞擊下無人生還。

02 *... after all.*
（畢竟……。）

Oscar takes all the responsibility for the class. He's the class leader after all.
奧斯卡擔下所有的責任，畢竟他是班長。

Common Sense 小常識

根據臉型挑衣服（2）

倒三角形臉：這種臉型也叫做瓜子臉，瓜子臉的人適合穿圓領或高領的衣服。
正三角形臉：這種臉型的人穿褶皺立領或收腰的衣服會更好看。
長形臉：這種臉型的人穿可愛的衣服更有魅力。
方形臉：方形臉女士穿柔和的衣服更有女人味。
菱形臉：菱形臉的人也適合穿高領或圓領的衣服。

Key Sentences 基本句大變身

track115

1	I want to buy a dress.	我想買條裙子。

- I need a dress. 我需要一條裙子。
- I'd like a dress. 我想買條裙子。

2	Yellow is too bright for me.	黃色對我來說太亮了。

- Yellow looks too loud. 黃色看起來太花俏了。
- Black is a bit too plain. 黑色有點太素了。

3	Do you have any other colors in this size?	這個尺寸還有其他顏色的嗎？

- Any other colors? 還有其他顏色的嗎？
- Do you have this size in red? 這個尺寸有紅色的嗎？

4	Does this color easy to fade?	這個顏色容易褪色嗎？

- Does the color of black fade easily? 黑色容易褪色嗎？
- Is white colorfast? 白色不會褪色嗎？

5	What material is the shirt made from?	這件襯衫是什麼材質？

- I need a shirt in wool. 我需要一件毛料的襯衫。
- Do you have this in cotton? 這種有棉質的嗎？

6	May I try it on?	我可以試試嗎？

- I want to try this on. 我想要試試這件。
- Where is the fitting room? 試衣間在哪裡？

7	I need a smaller size.	我需要再小一點的。

- I want a small / medium / large size. 我想要一個小／中／大號的。
- Can you take my measurements? 你能為我量一下嗎？

8	It fits me very well.	它很適合我。

- It's the right size for me. 這個尺寸剛好適合。
- It seems that this is made for me. 這好像就是為我做的。

45 Family & Digital Appliance 家用電器和數位產品

Dialogue 1 第一次聊就上手

track116

Salesclerk : What can I do for you, sir?

Tom : Yes. I want to buy a refrigerator which has double doors.

Salesclerk : I recommend this one for you. It's our best seller.

Tom : it looks great. Can I refund it if there's something wrong with its quality?

Salesclerk : Yes. You can refund it within six months.

Tom : That would be fine.

Translation 中譯照過來

售貨員：需要幫助嗎，先生？

湯　姆：是的，我想買一台雙開門冰箱。

售貨員：我會推薦這台。這是我們的暢銷商品。

湯　姆：它看起來很好。如果品質有問題的話我能退貨嗎？

售貨員：是的，半年內可以退貨。

湯　姆：那還好。

Key words 重點單字快速記

digital [ˋdɪdʒɪtḷ] 形. 數字的；數碼的
appliance [əˋplaɪəns] 名. 家用電器
refrigerator [rɪˋfrɪdʒəˏretɚ] 名. 冰箱
bestseller [bɛstˋsɛlɚ] 名. 暢銷產品
refund [ˋrɪˏfʌnd]
動. 退還（金額，尤因對所購貨物或服務不滿意）
quality [ˋkwɑlətɪ] 名. 品質

Patterns 延伸句型快速學

01 *... N which ....*
（具有……特徵的某物品。）

> Zack wants that new iPhone which has two camera lenses.
> 札克想要那台有兩個鏡頭的新 iPhone。

02 *... within* + 一段時間 .
（在……之內……。）

> The antibacterial test will be finished within two weeks.
> 那個抗菌測試會在二週內完成。

Common Sense 小常識

謹慎購買電器

在美國想要購買電器時一定要慎重考慮，因為大部分美國家電並沒有台灣先進，價錢也不比台灣便宜。美國的手機卻相對會便宜一點，因為美國的電信公司主要靠通話費收入來撐起營運，但手機款式會舊一些，沒有台灣的多變與花俏。

45 Family & Digital Appliance 家用電器和數位產品

Dialogue 2 第一次聊就上手

track117

Steven : I want to buy a new phone.

Salesclerk : How about a smart phone?

Steven : Isn't it too expensive?

Salesclerk : No, they become cheaper now?

Steven : Really?

Salesclerk : Look at this one. It is just 60 dollars.

Steven : I can't believe it.

Salesclerk : That's the trend.

Translation 中譯照過來

史蒂文：我想買個新手機。

售貨員：智慧型手機怎麼樣？

史蒂文：智慧型手機不是很貴嗎？

售貨員：不，現在便宜很多了。

史蒂文：真的嗎？

售貨員：看看這個。只要 60 美元。

史蒂文：我真不敢相信。

售貨員：這就是趨勢啊。

Key words 重點單字快速記

phone [fon] 名. 電話
smart [smɑrt] 形. （機器、武器、材料等）智能的
expensive [ɪk`spɛnsɪv] 形. 昂貴的，花錢多的
cheap [tʃip] 形. 便宜的，不貴的，廉價的
trend [trɛnd] 名. 趨勢，趨向

Patterns 延伸句型快速學

01 ***How about + N?***
（某物怎麼樣？）

How about a pizza for dinner?
來個比薩當晚餐如何？

02 ***S + become + adj.-er....***
（……變得更……。）

My kid becomes taller everyday.
我的孩子一天比一天變得更高。

Common Sense 小常識

謹慎購買電器

不管是哪一個國家，當地出產的品牌一定是在當地購買會便宜許多，而美國某些電器品牌，也是台灣人出國必般的商品之一，例如 Dyson 吸塵器、iPhone 手機等，但要注意的是，雖然撿了價格上的便宜，但有時候國外的貨品在台灣是無法享有保固的，這點在需要送原廠維修時會是一個很大的麻煩，所以在下手前還是要經過多方考慮跟評估才是。

Key Sentences 基本句大變身

track118

1	The cellphone comes with a lot of functions.	這個手機有很多功能。

- The cellphone has a lot of functions.
  這個手機有很多功能。

2	What are its functions?	它有哪些功能？

- What functions can it perform?
  它有哪些功能？
- What features does it have?
  它有什麼特點？

3	It's not rare to see people use smart phones.	使用智慧型手機的人並不少見。

- It's not rare to use mobile phones to watch TV series.
  用手機看電視劇並不罕見。

4	Is this freezer fluoride-free?	這個冰櫃是無氟的嗎？

- Is this refrigerator frost-free?
  這個冰箱是無霜的嗎？
- Do you have flouride-free refrigerator?
  你們有無氟冰箱嗎？

46 Discounted Goods 特價商品

Dialogue 1 第一次聊就上手

track119

Caroline : Are all the things on sale?

Salesclerk : Yes, we want to refurnish here.

Caroline : Is this a clearance sale?

Salesclerk : Exactly. You can take your time looking.

Caroline : That's great!

Translation 中譯照過來

卡洛琳：所有東西都在打折嗎？

售貨員：是啊，我們想重新裝修一下。

卡洛琳：這是清倉大拍賣嗎？

售貨員：正是如此。您慢慢看吧。

卡洛琳：太棒了！

Key words 重點單字快速記

discount [ˋdɪskaʊnt] 動. 打折扣，減價出售
goods [gʊdz] 名. 商品
sale [sel] 名. 拍賣
refurnish [rɪˋfɝnɪʃ] 動. 重新裝修
clearance [ˋklɪrəns] 名. 清除，清理

Patterns 延伸句型快速學

01 *... be on sale.*

（……特價中。）

Everything you see in the shop is on sale.
在店內你所看到的東西都在特價中。

02 *S + take sb's time + to V / Ving.*

（某人慢慢做……。）

Sam took his time driving back home.
山姆慢慢地開車回家。

Common Sense 小常識

美國的折扣商店

店名	範圍分布	商品	價格
Stein Mart	30 個州 263 家門市	女裝、男裝、配件、家居配飾、床單、鞋	比商店或專賣店價格低 40% 至 80%
Loehmann's	17 個州超過 50 家門市	女裝、男裝、鞋、配件、香水、禮品、緊身衣	比商店或專賣店價格低 30% 至 65%
Premium Outlets	24 個州 42 家門市	許多名牌商品，包括 BCBG Max Azria, Kenneth Cole, Ralph Lauren, Crate & Barrel, Burberry, Calvin Klein, Dior 等。	打折幅度很大

46 Discounted Goods 特價商品

Dialogue 2 第一次聊就上手

track120

Caroline : Look! Can you see that sign?

Bonnie : Which one?

Caroline : The one on the right. It seems that all the clothes are 80% off.

Bonnie : But this is a famous brand.

Caroline : Let's find out whether they are in good quality.

Translation 中譯照過來

卡洛琳：快看！你看到那個牌子了嗎？

邦　妮：哪個？

卡洛琳：右邊那個。看起來所有的衣服都打 2 折。

邦　妮：但這可是個名牌呢。

卡洛琳：我們去看看品質到底好不好。

Chapter1 交際篇
Chapter2 交通運輸篇
Chapter3 用餐事宜篇
Chapter4 愛情篇
Chapter5 校園生活篇
Chapter6 工作篇
Chapter7 購物篇
Chapter8 公共服務篇
Chapter9 情緒篇

Key words 重點單字快速記

sign [saɪn] 名. 標示
off [ɔf] 副. 削價，減價
famous [ˋfeməs] 形. 有名的
brand [brænd] 名. 品牌，牌子
whether [ˋhwɛðɚ] 連. 是否

Patterns 延伸句型快速學

01 *All + the N + are + ...*

（所有的東西都⋯⋯。）

All the watermelons here are over 5 kilograms.
這裡所有的西瓜都超過五公斤重。

02 *... whether S + V (+ O).*

（⋯⋯是否⋯⋯。）

I am wondering whether Upton is interested in this offer.
我不知道奧普敦是否會對這個提案感興趣。

Common Sense 小常識

美國的折扣商店

美國有許多大型的購物商場，裡面賣的東西很多都比一般商店便宜許多，且在 outlet 裡，更是幾乎每季；甚至每個月都有過季商品的促銷與拍賣。而每個不同的 outlet 也有著各自主打的熱賣促銷商品，想搶便宜的人可以在平常就多多比較各家釋出的優惠訊息，當個聰明的購物高手喔！

Key Sentences 基本句大變身

track121

1 Are you sure this dress is 50% off? 你確定這條裙子半價？

- Are you sure this dress is discounted 50%?
  你確定這條裙子半價？
- Are you sure this dress allow 50% discounts?
  你確定這條裙子半價？

2 There is a discount on the jewelry. 珠寶在打折。

- This jewelry will be sold at a discount.
  這件珠寶將減價出售。

3 I can't believe this shirt is so cheap. 真不敢相信這件襯衫居然這麼便宜。

- It is unbelievable that this shirt is so cheap.
  真不敢相信這件襯衫居然這麼便宜。
- I still doubt this shirt is so cheap.
  我還是不相信這件襯衫居然這麼便宜。

4 Is there a discount? 有折扣嗎？

- Is this one on sale?
  這件在特價嗎？
- Any discount on this?
  這個有打折嗎？

47 Bargaining 討價還價

Dialogue 1 第一次聊就上手

track122

Bonnie : I'd buy it at once if the price can be cheaper.

Salesclerk : I can give you a 20% discount.

Bonnie : That won't make any difference. What about a 30% (discount)?

Salesclerk : No, I won't make any money. Take it or leave it.

Bonnie : OK. See you.

Translation 中譯照過來

邦　妮：要是你能再便宜一點，我馬上就買。

售貨員：我可以給你打個八折。

邦　妮：那也沒什麼區別啊。打個七折怎麼樣？

售貨員：不行，這樣我就沒有賺了。不滿意就算了。

邦　妮：好吧。再見。

Key words 重點單字快速記

bargaining [ˋbɑrgɪnɪŋ] 名. 討價還價；談條件
cheaper [ˋtʃipɚ] 形. 更便宜的
difference [ˋdɪfərəns] 名. 差別，差異
take [tek] 動. 接受（某人給的東西、提議等）
money [ˋmʌnɪ] 名. 金錢

Patterns 延伸句型快速學

01 ***... at once ....***
（……馬上……。）

When the class takes a short break, Norman eats 5 cupcakes at once.
當課間短暫的休息時間一到，諾曼馬上吃了五個杯子蛋糕。

02 ***S + give + O1 + O2.***
（某人給予某人某物。）

My sister gives me her new laptop.
我姐姐給了我她的新筆記型電腦。

Common Sense 小常識

美國的免稅州（1）

美國有 5 個州的政府是不對任何商品收稅的，它們分別是：奧勒岡州（Oregon）、阿拉斯加州（Alaska）、德拉瓦州（Delaware）、蒙大拿州（Montana）和新罕布夏州（New Hampshire）。

47 Bargaining 討價還價

Dialogue 2 第一次聊就上手

track123

Caroline : It's worth 30 dollars at most.

Salesclerk : No way! It cost me more than that. One hundred dollars.

Caroline : Come on! I will not buy this if you don't lower the price.

Salesclerk : Eighty dollars. Accept it or reject it.

Caroline : I can only give you 60 dollars.

Salesclerk : Alright, I'll let you have it for 60 dollars.

Translation 中譯照過來

卡洛琳：它最多值 30 美元。

售貨員：不可能！我的進價都比這個價高。100 美元。

卡洛琳：少來了！你要是不便宜點我就不買了。

售貨員：80 美元。不買就算了。

卡洛琳：我只給你 60 美元。

售貨員：好吧，就 60 美元賣給你吧。

Key words 重點單字快速記

cost [kɔst] 動. 花費
lower [`loɚ] 動. 減少，降低
accept [ək`sɛpt] 動.（認為符合要求而）接受
reject [rɪ`dʒɛkt] 動. 拒絕接受
alright [`ɔl`raɪt] 形. 沒問題

Patterns 延伸句型快速學

01 ***Sth + be + worth +*** **金額 .**
（某物值……元。）

> Your bike is worth nothing.
> 你的腳踏車一點都不值錢。

02 ***Sth + cost / costs + sb +*** **金額 .**
（某物花了某人……元。）

> My watch cost me 800,000 dollars.
> 我的手錶花了我八十萬元。

Common Sense 小常識

美國的免稅州（2）

雖然上述提到的 5 個州不對商品收稅，但這些免稅州的地方政府可能會徵收一些消費稅。此外，美國紐澤西州（New Jersey）則是部分的商品免稅。

Key Sentences 基本句大變身

track124

1 Take it or leave it. 買不買隨便你。

- It's the best offer I can make. Take it or leave it.
  這是我能給的最低價了。買不買隨便你。
- Accept it or reject it.
  不滿意就算了。
- Be satisfied with it or get nothing.
  不滿意就算了。

2 I'll give 50 dollars for it. 我出 50 美元買它。

- I'll buy it for 50 dollars.
  我出 50 美元買它。
- I'll get it for 50 dollars.
  我出 50 美元買它。

3 I'd buy it at once if the price can be cheaper. 便宜一點的話我馬上就買。

- I'd buy it at once if it were not so expensive.
  如果不這麼貴的話我馬上就買。
- I'd buy it right away if it were inexpensive.
  如果不這麼貴的話我馬上就買。

4 Could it be less expensive? 能便宜一點嗎？

- Could it be cheaper?
  能便宜一點嗎？
- Can you make it cheaper?
  能便宜一點嗎？

48 After-sales Service 售後服務

Dialogue 1 第一次聊就上手

track125

Bonnie : Look! There is a slit on the dress!

Salesclerk : Can you make sure that it was bought like this?

Bonnie : Yes, I never put it on.

Salesclerk : OK. I will change it for you.

Bonnie : Thank you very much.

Translation 中譯照過來

邦　妮：看！裙子上有道裂縫！

售貨員：你確定買的時候就是這樣？

邦　妮：是啊，我都沒穿過呢！

售貨員：好的，我會給你換一件的。

邦　妮：非常感謝你。

Key words 重點單字快速記

after [ˋæftɚ] 連. 在……之後
service [ˋsɝvɪs] 名. 服務
slit [slɪt] 名. 狹長的切口
sure [ʃʊr] 形. 確定
change [tʃendʒ] 動. 更換

Patterns 延伸句型快速學

01 *There + be + N + ...*

（有……。）

> There are at least 3 emergency exits on a bus.
> 在巴士上至少有三個緊急出口。

02 *Can you make sure that....*

（你能確認……嗎？）

> Can you make sure that the flight will be arriving on time?
> 你能確認班機會準時抵達嗎？

Common Sense 小常識

美元

美元紙幣面額分為 100、50、20、10、5、2、1 美元；硬幣分為 50、25、10、5、1 美分和 1 美元。美元正面是著名人物頭像，反面則通常為著名建築物，但根據發行的時間而略有不同。

Key Sentences 基本句大變身

track126

1 I need a refund, please. 請退我錢。

- Give my money back, please.
  請把我的錢退給我。
- Can I have a refund?
  能退款給我嗎？

2 The damage is your fault. 這個損壞是你們的責任。

- You are responsible for the damage.
  你們要對損壞負責。
- You should answer for the damage.
  你們要對損壞負責。

3 Is the damage serious? 損壞很嚴重嗎？

- How serious is the damage?
  損壞情況有多嚴重？

4 Can I return it if it doesn't work? 如果不能用的話，我能退貨嗎？

- Can I bring it back if it doesn't work?
  如果沒有效果的話我可以把它退回來嗎？

KNESS—A T IN
D FOR THE BEDSIDE LAMP AND TURNED IT
UINTING AT HIS SURROU
S, AND A COLOSSAL MAHOGANY FO
ILIAR RING. PI
ROOM WITH LOUIS XVI FURE, HAND-FRE S
SCOUR-POSTER BED.LA
HONE WAS RINGING IN THE A
D FOR THE BEDSIDE LAMP AND TURNED IT
UINTING AT HIS SURROU
S, AND A COLOSSAL MAHOGANY FO
ROOM WITH LOUIS XVI FURE, HAND-FRE S
SCOUR-POSTER BED.LA
IDE TABLE.TH
ON A CRUMPLED FLYER ON
OUDLY PRESENTSA
GDON PROFESSOR O
Y. A VISITOR? HIS EYES FOC
BCAN UNIVERSITY OF
RIN EVENING
GIOUS SYMBOLOGY, HARV
NIVERSITY LANGDO

Chapter 8

Public Service

公共服務篇

49 At the Post Office 在郵局

Dialogue 1 第一次聊就上手

track127

Steven : Hello, I come here to pick up my package from China.

Postal clerk : Have you brought the receipt with you?

Steven : Yes, here you are.

Postal clerk : And you should show me your ID card.

Steven : Sure, here is my ID card.

Postal clerk : OK. I'll get it for you.

Steven : Thank you.

Translation 中譯照過來

史 蒂 文：你好，我來取從中國寄來的包裹。

郵局職員：你帶收據了嗎？

史 蒂 文：帶了，給你。

郵局職員：你要給我看一下你的身分證。

史 蒂 文：好的，在這裡。

郵局職員：好的。我去幫你拿。

史 蒂 文：謝謝你。

Key words 重點單字快速記

public [ˋpʌblɪk] 形. 公眾的
post [post] 名. 崗位
package [ˋpækɪdʒ] 名. 包裹
from [frɑm] 介. 從……來
receipt [rɪˋsit] 名. 收據

Patterns 延伸句型快速學

01 ***pick up + N.***
（取走……。）

> Clark was here to pick up the sweater he left yesterday.
> 克拉克來取走他昨天遺留下的毛衣。

02 ***Sb + bring + N + with + sb.***
（某人帶著……。）

> Adolf brings his bat with him to the baseball field.
> 阿道夫帶著他的球棒到棒球場去了。

Common Sense 小常識

穩定的通訊地址很重要（1）

在美國，如果想要及時、準確地獲得移民身分等重要文件，就一定要有穩定的通訊地址，否則一旦出現延遲回覆或其他延遲的狀況，往往會導致各個步驟都推遲延誤，這也是那些期盼早日解決移民問題的人最不願看到的結果。後面我們會提到應該如何避免！

49 At the Post Office 在郵局

Dialogue 2 第一次聊就上手

track128

Postal clerk : What can I do for you?

Anna : I'd like to deliver this package to New York.

Postal clerk : OK, you need to fill in this form.

Anna : Sure. Can you tell me the zip code of New York City?

Postal clerk : Yes. It's 10001 NY 212.

Anna : Thanks. Here you go.

Translation 中譯照過來

郵局職員：我可以為你做點什麼嗎？

安　　娜：我想把這個包裹寄到紐約。

郵局職員：好的，你需要填一下這張表格。

安　　娜：好的。你能告訴我紐約市的郵政編號嗎？

郵局職員：好的。是 10001 NY 212。

安　　娜：謝謝。給你

Key words 重點單字快速記

deliver [dɪˋlɪvɚ] 動. 遞送，傳送

need [nid] 名. 需要

fill [fɪl] 動. 填滿

form [fɔrm] 名. 表格

zip [zɪp] 名. 此處與 code 連用，為郵政編碼之意

Patterns 延伸句型快速學

01 *fill in + N.*

（填寫……。）

> We need to fill in the work sheet after we finish our shift.
> 我們要在輪班完後填寫工作表格。

02 *Can you tell me (that) ...?*

（你能告訴我……嗎？）

> Can you tell me which team is taking the lead now?
> 你能告訴我現在哪一隊領先嗎？

Common Sense 小常識

穩定的通訊地址很重要（2）

作為新移民該怎麼避免政府機關重要文件延遲的發生呢？

1. 剛剛入境的移民，尤其英文讀寫能力稍微不好的人，建議繼續使用區域中心的地址。
2. 在自己居住地所屬郵局租個郵件箱。
3. 把自己的現住的地址設為通訊地址，並且將該地址通知給移民局。

Key Sentences 基本句大變身

track129

1	How would you like to send it?	您想怎麼寄？

- How would you like it to go?
  你想怎麼寄？
- Where would you like to send it?
  您想把它寄到哪裡？

2	Do you want it insured?	你想幫它（該物品）保險嗎？

- Do you want it registered?
  你想寄掛號嗎？
- Would you like to send it by express mail?
  你想用快遞寄送嗎？

3	I come here to pick up my package.	我來取我的包裹。

- I come here to get my package.
  我來拿我的包裹。

4	What's the postage for special delivery?	快遞的郵資是多少？

- What's the postage for surface mail?
  普通的郵資是多少？
- What is the postage on this package?
  寄這個包裹郵資是多少？

50 At the Bank 在銀行

Dialogue 1 第一次聊就上手

track130

Mary : Excuse me? I want to open a checking account.

Bank clerk : OK. Please show me your ID card, and then you have to fill out this form.

Mary : Here is my ID card. Can you tell me the minimum amount I can deposit in?

Bank clerk : Ten dollars.

Mary : Thank you.

Translation 中譯照過來

瑪　　麗：打擾一下，我想開個活期帳戶。

銀行職員：好的。請給我看一下你的身分證，然後你得填一下這張表格。

瑪　　麗：這是我的身分證。你能告訴我必須存入的最小金額是多少嗎？

銀行職員：10 美元。

瑪　　麗：謝謝你。

Key words 重點單字快速記

bank [bæŋk] 名. 銀行
checking [tʃɛkɪŋ] 名. 支票
account [ə`kaʊnt] 名. 帳戶
minimum [`mɪnəməm] 形. 最少的；最低限度的
amount [ə`maʊnt] 名. 數額，數量
deposit [dɪ`pɑzɪt]
動. 將（錢或貴重物品）存入（銀行或其他安全的地方）

Patterns 延伸句型快速學

01 *I want to V + ...*

（我想要……。）

> I want to buy you a new shirt.
> 我想要幫你買件新衣服。

02 *..., and then....*

（……，然後……。）

> My daddy is going to pick up my sister first, and then coming for me.
> 我爸爸要先去接我的妹妹，然後才來接我。

Common Sense 小常識

美國人的理財方式（1）

作為高消費國家的人民，美國人極少使用現金消費，大多數情況下他們更願意使用支票或信用卡，因此，去銀行領錢的人寥寥無幾。美國人消費思想較為超前，又習慣使用信用卡，因此他們會比我們更有機會出現信用卡透支或助學貸款還不起，畢業即破產等現象。

50 At the Bank 在銀行

Dialogue 2 第一次聊就上手

track131

Kenny : Can you help me to change 200 dollars into RMB?

Bank clerk : Certainly.

Kenny : What is the exchange rate today?

Bank clerk : One US dollar to 6.20 RMB. Is that OK?

Kenny : Yes, please.

Translation 中譯照過來

肯　　尼：你能幫我把 200 美元兑換成人民幣嗎？
銀行職員：當然可以。
肯　　尼：今天的匯率是多少？
銀行職員：1 美元兑 6.20 元人民幣，可以嗎？
肯　　尼：可以。

Key words 重點單字快速記

dollar [ˋdalɚ] 名. 美元
certainly [ˋsɝtənlɪ] 副. 必然地；確實地
exchange [ɪksˋtʃendʒ] 名. （貨幣的）兑換
rate [ret] 名. 比率，匯率
please [pliz] 動. 請

Patterns 延伸句型快速學

01 *Can you help me (to) V...?*
（你能幫我……嗎？）

> Can you help me drag this bag to the hilltop?
> 你能幫我把這袋子拖到山上嗎？

02 *change A to B.*
（把 A 換成 B。）

> I want to change the shirt from M size to L size.
> 我想把這件衣服從 M 號換成 L 號。

Common Sense 小常識

美國人的理財方式（2）

前面提過的可能會透支的風險並不會影響美國人的金錢觀，他們仍然常常會借錢出去遊玩。隨著年齡的增長，美國人也會為自己的老年生活存錢，有的還會投資基金或股票等來為自己賺錢。因此，美國人的理財有三個時期：消費期、節省期和養老期。

Key 基本句大變身 Sentences

track132

1 I'd like to open a saving account. 我想開個儲蓄帳戶。

- I'd like to open a checking account.
  我想開個活期帳戶。
- Is there a service charge for the checking account?
  開支票帳戶要收服務費嗎？

2 I want to pay 100 dollars into my account. 我想存 100 美元到我的帳戶裡。

- I want to pay all the money into my account.
  我想把所有這些錢存入我的帳戶裡。
- I want to deposit the money into my account.
  我想把錢存進我的帳戶裡。

3 What's the exchange rate for RMB? 人民幣的兌換匯率是多少？

- What's the RMB going for today?
  今天人民幣的售價是多少？
- What's the rate of exchange between pound and the US dollar?
  英鎊和美元的匯率是多少？
- The exchange rate today is 1 pound to 1.56 US dollars.
  今天 1 英鎊兌換 1.56 美元。

4 I want to change 1,000 pounds for dollars. 我想把 1,000 英鎊兌換成美元。

- What do you want to change for?
  您想要換什麼？
- How much do you want to exchange?
  你想兌換多少？
- How much would I get for 10,000 Japanese yen?
  一萬日元可以兌換多少？

51 At the Police Station 在警察局

Dialogue 1 第一次聊就上手

track133

April: Can you help me, sir? My wallet was lost.

Police: Can you describe the trait of the wallet?

April: It's a small one, pink leather with a flower on it.

Police: What's in it?

April: My ID card, credit card, and more than 300 dollars.

Police: OK. You need to fill out this form and we'll contact you when we find it.

April: Thank you.

Translation 中譯照過來

阿普裏爾：先生，您能幫助我嗎？我的錢包遺失了。

警　　察：你能描述一下錢包的特徵嗎？

阿普裏爾：是個粉紅色皮革的小錢包，上面有花朵裝飾。

警　　察：裡面有什麼東西呢？

阿普裏爾：我的身分證、信用卡，還有 300 多美元。

警　　察：好的。你需要填寫一下這張表格。我們找到以後會跟你聯繫的。

阿普裏爾：謝謝你。

Key words 重點單字快速記

wallet [ˋwɑlɪt] 名. 錢包
describe [dɪˋskraɪb] 動. 描述，描寫
trait [tret] 名. 特性，品質
leather [ˋlɛðɚ] 名. 皮革
contact [ˋkɑntækt] 動. （寫信、打電話）聯繫（某人）

Patterns 延伸句型快速學

01 *N was lost.*

（……遺失了。）

> Tiffany's cat was lost.
> 蒂芬尼的貓遺失了。

02 *S + will + V (+ O) when S + V (+ O).*

（當……後，將……。）

> The post office will inform me when my package arrives.
> 當我的包裹寄到了以後，郵局將會通知我。

Common Sense 小常識

夫妻吵架也要進警察局（1）

在台灣，夫妻吵架鬥嘴是常有的事，甚至一對男女在大街上拉拉扯扯也不足為奇。但這樣的事如果在美國發生，一定會有路人去報警並充當證人。即便在家爭執受傷去醫院看病，醫生也會報警。打人的一方會被警察關押 1 ～ 3 天，並等待法官發落，與此同時還要繳納上千美金才可以被釋放。

51 At the Police Station 在警察局

Dialogue 2 第一次聊就上手

track134

Mike : Excuse me, sir? Someone stole my car this morning.

Police : Where did you park it?

Mike : I parked it just outside my house last night. But it was gone this morning.

Police : Can you tell me your license plate number?

Mike : C-12345.

Police : And what's your car's color and brand?

Mike : It's a black Audi.

Police : OK. We'll get into investigation in an hour.

Translation 中譯照過來

邁克：打擾了先生，今天早上有人偷了我的車。

警察：你把它停在哪裡呢？

邁克：昨天晚上我就把車停在我家外面，但今天早上就不見了。

警察：你能告訴我車牌號碼是多少嗎？

邁克：C-12345。

警察：你的車是什麼顏色、什麼牌子的？

邁克：是輛黑色的奧迪。

警察：好的。我們會在一小時內展開調查。

Key words 重點單字快速記

steal [stil] 動 偷竊
car [kɑr] 名 車子
park [pɑrk] 動 停車
outside [ˋaʊtˋsaɪd] 名 室外
investigation [ɪnˏvɛstəˋgeʃən] 名 調查

Patterns 延伸句型快速學

01 ***N was gone.***
（……不見了。）

My cookies were gone!
我的餅乾不見了！

02 ***get into + N.***
（進入……（的狀態）。）

Wilson kept silence for not getting into trouble.
威爾森保持沈默，以避免惹上麻煩。

Common Sense 小常識

夫妻吵架也要進警察局（2）

夫妻吵架進了警局，被釋放後也不代表就可以回家了，法官會發給被打的一方保護令；其中有一種保護令規定，打人的一方雖然可以回家，但不能威脅被打者，否則還會被抓。而另一種保護令，則是會規定打人者在一定時間範圍內禁止回家，甚至不能以任何方式聯繫被打者，若被打者沒有經濟收入，打人者還要為其提供生活費。

Key Sentences 基本句大變身

track135

1 Can we ask you some questions? 我們能問你幾個問題嗎？

- We have a few questions to ask you.
  我們有幾個問題想要問你。
- I just need to ask you a few questions.
  我只需要問你幾個問題。

2 I have taken down the case. 我已經把情況記錄下來了。

- I have taken down witness's statement.
  我已經把目擊者所說的記錄下來了。

3 It will be dealt with at once. 我們會馬上處理的。

- We will start the investigation swiftly.
  我們會迅速展開調查的。
- We will look into the matter immediately.
  我們會馬上調查此事。

4 Can you identify the suspect? 你能認出嫌犯嗎？

- Can you identify who attacked you?
  你能認出是誰襲擊的你嗎？
- Can you give a description of the attacker?
  你能描述一下襲擊者嗎？

52 In the Hospital 在醫院

Dialogue 1 第一次聊就上手

track136

Doctor : What's wrong with you?

Jack : I have got a stomachache. Maybe it was because I ate too much last night.

Doctor : Did you vomited last night?

Jack : Yes, I vomited twice, and I also have loose bowels.

Doctor : You need to get your stools tested, and then bring the report to me.

Jack : OK. Thank you.

Translation 中譯照過來

醫生：你怎麼了？

傑克：我胃痛。可能是昨晚吃得太多了。

醫生：你昨天晚上有吐嗎？

傑克：是的，昨晚吐了兩次，而且還拉肚子。

醫生：你必須做一次糞便檢查。然後把化驗報告給我。

傑克：好的。謝謝。

Key words 重點單字快速記

hospital [ˋhɑspɪtl̩] 名. 醫院
stomachache [ˋstʌməkˏek] 名. 胃痛；肚子痛
vomit [ˋvɑmɪt] 動. 嘔吐
bowel [ˋbaʊəl] 名. 腸
stool [stul] 名. 大便，糞便
report [rɪˋport] 名. 報告

Patterns 延伸句型快速學

01 *S + have / has got a ....*

（犯了……（疾病）。）

Ingrid has got a diarrhea.
英格蒂犯了腹瀉。

02 *get + O + pp..*

（使……（被）……。）

Pat gets his pitbull well contained.
派特使他的比特犬被好好的關著。

Common Sense 小常識

美國醫院

美國醫院有公立的也有私立的，公立醫院通常屬於綜合性醫院，而私立醫院則屬於專科醫院。美國也有社區診所，但社區診所多數只是為病人進行最基礎的檢查和初檢，對病情作出初步判定。因此，大多數美國人都願意花錢購買醫療保險，這樣一旦生病去醫院，就可以省下很大一部分開支。

Key Sentences 基本句大變身

track137

1 What's wrong with you? 怎麼了？

- What's the matter?
  怎麼了？
- Is anything wrong?
  哪裡不舒服嗎？

2 Let me check your temperature. 讓我幫你量一下體溫。

- Let me check your blood pressure.
  讓我幫你量一下血壓。

3 I have a headache. 我頭痛。

- My head hurts.
  我頭痛。
- My head is pounding.
  我頭痛。

4 Are you alright again? 你的病好了嗎？

- Are you yourself again?
  你好了嗎？
- Are you back to normal again?
  你恢復正常了嗎？

53 In the Museum 在博物館

Dialogue 1 第一次聊就上手

track138

Museum worker : Sorry, we are going to close today.

Jean : What time does the museum close?

Museum worker : At 5:00 pm.

Jean : Then what time does it open tomorrow?

Museum worker : At 10:00 am.

Jean : Can you tell me how much is the admission?

Museum worker : Certainly. Ten dollars for an adult and five dollars for a student.

Jean : I see. Thank you.

Translation 中譯照過來

博物館工作人員：對不起，我們今天要閉館了。

瓊：什麼時候閉館？

博物館工作人員：下午 5 點。

瓊：那明天什麼時候開館呢？

博物館工作人員：上午 10 點開館。

瓊：你能告訴我門票是多少錢嗎？

博物館工作人員：當然。成人一張 10 美元，學生一張 5 美元。

瓊：我知道了。謝謝。

Key words 重點單字快速記

museum [mjuˋzɪəm] 名. 博物館
open [ˋopən] 動. 營業；打開
admission [ədˋmɪʃən] 名. 入場費
adult [əˋdʌlt] 名. 成年人
student [ˋstjudn̩t] 名. 學生

Patterns 延伸句型快速學

01 ***What time + aux. + S + V?***
（什麼時間……？）

What time does the library open?
圖書館幾點開？

02 ***How much + be + sth?***
（某物多少錢？）

How much is your new laptop?
你的新筆記型電腦多少錢？

Common Sense 小常識

美國非比尋常的博物館（1）

波士頓——糟糕藝術博物館：收藏了藝術家的失誤之作。
費城——穆特爾醫學史博物館：收藏了上千個解剖和病理學標本。
維吉尼亞州——亞歷山大藥材博物館：收藏了醫藥史上具有重要意義的器具和物品。
威斯康辛州——芥末博物館：收集了來自 70 多個國家的 5,000 多罐芥末，在吧檯可以免費試吃多種不同的口味。

53 In the Museum 在博物館

Dialogue 2 第一次聊就上手

track139

Tyler : Have you got the tickets?

Cassie : Yes. That's so expensive.

Tyler : You know, this is the busy season.

Cassie : Well. What is on show now?

Tyler : Some objects from Tang Dynasty.

Cassie : I hope it's worth the money.

Translation 中譯照過來

泰勒：你買到票了嗎？

凱西：買到了。好貴啊。

泰勒：你知道的，現在正是旺季。

凱西：好吧。現在在展出什麼？

泰勒：一些唐朝時期的藝術品。

凱西：希望能物有所值。

Key words 重點單字快速記

ticket [ˋtɪkɪt] 名. 票券

expensive [ɪkˋspɛnsɪv] 形. 昂貴的

season [ˋsizn̩] 名. 季節

show [ʃo] 名. 展示

object [ˋɑbdʒɪkt] 名. 物品

Patterns 延伸句型快速學

01 *You know, ...*

（你知道的，……。）

> You know, this is the way it is.
> 你知道的，這就是如此。

02 *... be on show.*

（……展示中。）

> Da Vinci's paintings and sculptures are on show now at the National Museum.
> 達文齊的畫作與雕塑正在國家博物館展示中。

Common Sense 小常識

美國非比尋常的博物館（2）

加利福尼亞州——伯林蓋姆皮禮士糖果盒（Pez）博物館：收集了各式各樣的皮禮士糖果盒，這個袖珍博物館收集了世界上最大的皮禮士糖果自動售賣機。

密蘇里州——頭髮博物館：收藏了許多用人的頭髮做成的精美藝術品。

新墨西哥州——羅斯威爾不明飛行物博物館：展出與實體外星人和飛碟同等比例的模型。

德克薩斯州——麥克萊恩鐵絲網博物館：收藏了超過 2,000 種各不相同的鐵絲網。

Key Sentences 基本句大變身

track140

1 Are there any exhibitions on now? 現在有什麼展覽嗎？

- Are there any special exhibitions being held now?
  現在有什麼特別展覽嗎？

2 The exhibition is open to the public. 這個展覽是公開的。

- The exhibition is open to the adults only.
  展覽只向成人開放。
- The museum is closed to visitors on Mondays.
  博物館週一不對參觀者開放。

3 What age was this object in? 這個展示品是什麼年代的？

- The permanent works focus on British masterpieces from the 16th to late 20th centuries.
  固定的展示品主要是英國 16 世紀到 20 世紀末期間的傑作。

4 Our opening hour is from 10:00 am to 5:00 pm. 我們的開館時間是上午 10 點到下午 5 點。

- We open from 10:00 am to 5:00 pm everyday throughout the year.
  我們全年都是每天上午 10 點至下午 5 點開放。
- The works are on show at the museum until October.
  這些作品會在博物館展出到 10 月。

54 In the Gym 在健身房

Dialogue 1 第一次聊就上手

track141

Elena : I didn't know you could exercise.

Matt : What do you mean by saying that?

Elena : I mean you are not like those who like doing exercise.

Matt : Not at all. I'd like to do some running.

Elena : Oh, I can't imagine you running.

Matt : I have to, because I need to get in shape.

Elena : That's true. If people don't exercise, they get sluggish.

Translation 中譯照過來

埃琳娜：我都不知道你會運動。

馬　特：你這麼說是什麼意思啊？

埃琳娜：我是說你不像那種喜歡運動的人。

馬　特：並不是！我喜歡跑步。

埃琳娜：噢，我無法想像你跑步的樣子。

馬　特：我不得不這樣，因為我需要保持身材。

埃琳娜：這倒是真的。人要是不運動，就會變得遲緩。

Chapter1 交際篇
Chapter2 交通運輸篇
Chapter3 用餐事宜篇
Chapter4 愛情篇
Chapter5 校園生活篇
Chapter6 工作篇
Chapter7 購物篇
Chapter8 公共服務篇
Chapter9 情緒篇

Key words 重點單字快速記

gym [dʒɪm] 名. 體育館，健身房
exercise [ˋɛksɚ͵saɪz] 名. 運動，鍛煉
run [rʌn] 動. 跑步
imagine [ɪˋmædʒɪn] 動. 想像
sluggish [ˋslʌgɪʃ] 形. 行動緩慢的，反應遲緩的；懶惰的

Patterns 延伸句型快速學

01 *S + be (not) like + N.*
（……（不）像……。）

George is not like a quitter.
喬治不像是個半途而廢的人。

02 *I can't imaging + O + Ving.*
（我無法想像……（做某事）。）

I can't imagine Sandy teaching.
我無法想像珊迪教書。

Common Sense 小常識

台灣人及美國人在運動上的觀念差異（1）

年齡	美國	台灣
5-8 歲	由父母帶領著接觸運動項目	在家念書
9-12 歲	幾乎每天都會有出去運動的時間	學校課業繁忙，根本沒時間運動
13-14 歲	喜歡運動帶來的樂趣	普遍不喜歡運動
15-18 歲	開始會有想專注鍛鍊的部位	為考試奮鬥熬夜，不會有多餘的時間運動
19-25 歲	健身是生活的一部分	為工作而奔波，除非為了瘦身否則基本上不會特別去運動

54 In the Gym 在健身房

Dialogue 2 第一次聊就上手

track142

Stefan : What can I do for you, madam?

Elena : Well, I want to do some exercise to keep fit.

Stefan : OK. First of all, we'll design a custom-made work out plan according to your habits.

Elena : That sounds great, but how?

Stefan : We will assign a qualified personal trainer to you.

Elena : That's great. I'll have a try.

Translation 中譯照過來

斯蒂芬：女士，有什麼能為您效勞的嗎？

埃琳娜：是的，我想要做點運動來保持體型。

斯蒂芬：好的。首先，我們會根據您的習慣為您量身訂製一個健身計劃。

埃琳娜：聽起來很棒，但是怎麼做呢？

斯蒂芬：我們會為您安排一名專業的私人健身教練。

埃琳娜：太棒了。那我會試試看。

Key words 重點單字快速記

design [dɪˋzaɪn] 動.（為某種特定目的）計劃，設計
workout [ˋwɝkˏaut] 名.（尤指體育）鍛煉，訓練
habit [ˋhæbɪt] 名. 習慣
assign [əˋsaɪn] 動. 分配，分派
qualified [ˋkwɑləˏfaɪd] 形.
（尤指做某項工作）有資格的，合格的，勝任的
trainer [ˋtrenɚ] 名. 教練

Patterns 延伸句型快速學

01 ***First of all, ...***
（首先，……。）

> First of all, you have to shave before meeting your girl.
> 首先，你要在去跟女朋友約會前刮鬍子。

02 ***S + V (+ O) + according to + N.***
（根據……。）

> The teacher will set a goal according to students' performance, respectively.
> 老師會依據學生個別的表現設定目標。

Common Sense 小常識

台灣人及美國人在運動上的觀念差異（2）

雖然前述對於台灣人運動習慣的說法看似有些極端，但卻的確是大部分人的現狀。在美國，運動這件事則是被教育者們看做是「教育」的一環，孩子們從小就可以從玩樂性質的運動中學習團隊合作、不卑不亢及靈活運用自己身體的方法，這也與美國人較為外向、熱情的人格特質有著相輔相成的關係。

Key Sentences 基本句大變身

track143

1	I need to do a workout.	我需要去鍛鍊一下。

- I plan to do a workout.
  我計畫去鍛鍊一下。
- I got to start exercising.
  我要開始鍛鍊了。

2	I think a little exercise will be good for you.	我覺得做點運動對你有好處。

- I think a little exercise will do you good.
  我覺得做點運動對你有好處。
- Proper exercise is good for your health.
  適度的鍛鍊對你的身體有好處。

3	It is a good idea to join a fitness center.	參加健身俱樂部是個好主意。

- It is good for you to join a fitness center.
  參加健身俱樂部對你有好處。
- It is a good choice for you to join a fitness center.
  參加健身俱樂部對你來說是個不錯的選擇。

4	She runs every day for purpose of being strong.	為了變強壯，她每天都跑步。

- For purpose of being strong, she runs every day.
  為了變強壯，她每天都跑步。
- For the sake of good health, we need to keep the trim figure.
  為了健康，我們要保持身材勻稱。

55 In the Cinema 在電影院

Dialogue 1 第一次聊就上手

track144

John : How about going to see a movie together?

Ann : What's on?

John : Avatar.

Ann : I've been looking forward to seeing it. When does it start?

John : It starts at 8 pm.

Ann : It's already 7 now. Let's have a quick dinner and go.

John : OK.

Translation 中譯照過來

約翰：一起去看電影怎麼樣？

安：什麼電影啊？

約翰：《阿凡達》。

安：我早就想看這部電影了。什麼時候開始？

約翰：下午 8 點。

安：現在都已經 7 點了。我們快點吃完飯就去吧。

約翰：好的。

Key words 重點單字快速記

cinema [ˋsɪnəmə] 名. 電影院
movie [ˋmuvɪ] 名. 電影
together [təˋgɛðɚ] 副. 一起
start [stɑrt] 動. 開始
quick [kwɪk] 形. 快速的

Patterns 延伸句型快速學

01 *S + look forward to + Ving.*
（……期待（做）……。）

Sam and Olivia have been looking forward to camping.
山姆和奧利維雅很期待去露營。

02 *N + start at +* 時間點 *.*
（……在……（時間點）開始。）

The movie starts at 9 pm tonight on HBO.
電影今晚九點在 HBO 開始放映。

Common Sense 小常識

美國電影級別（1）

G 級：大眾級，適合所有年齡層的人觀看。
PG 級：輔導級，部分內容可能不適合兒童觀看。
PG-13 級：特別輔導級，適合 13 歲以上人群觀看。

55 In the Cinema 在電影院

Dialogue 2 第一次聊就上手

track145

John : What are you going to do tonight?

Elena : I'm going to watch the Oscar Ceremony at home.

John : What's it about?

Elena : It's a ceremony hold to give the awards to the out standing movies and their staff.

John : Who do you think will win the award this year?

Elena : It's hard to say.

Translation 中譯照過來

約　翰：今晚你打算做什麼？

埃琳娜：我準備在家看奧斯卡頒獎典禮。

約　翰：它是關於什麼的？

埃琳娜：它是給傑出的電影和電影從業人員頒獎的一個典禮。

約　翰：那你覺得今年誰會獲獎？

埃琳娜：不好說。

Key words 重點單字快速記

Oscar [ˋɔskɚ] 名. 奧斯卡金像獎（一年一度的美國電影獎）
ceremony [ˋsɛrə͵monɪ] 名. 典禮，儀式
award [əˋwɔrd] 名. 獎，獎賞
outstanding [ˋautˋstændɪŋ] 形. 傑出的，優秀的，出色的
staff [stæf] 名. 工作人員

Patterns 延伸句型快速學

01 ***S + give + sth + to + sb.***
（……給某人某物。）

Ursula gave her book to me.
烏蘇拉把她的書給了我。

02 ***Who do you think will + V...?***
（你認為誰將會……呢？）

Who do you think will win the race this weekend?
你覺得週末的比賽誰會贏？

Common Sense 小常識

美國電影級別（2）

R 級：限制級，17 歲以下必須由父母或者監護人陪伴才能觀看。

NC-17 級：特別限制級，17 歲以下觀眾禁止觀看。

Key Sentences 基本句大變身

track146

1 How do you feel about the movie? 你覺得這部電影怎麼樣？

- How do you like the movie?
  你覺得這部電影怎麼樣？
- What do you think of the movie?
  你覺得這部電影怎麼樣？

2 I wonder if we can see a comedy. 我在想我們是否可以看喜劇。

- I don't feel like seeing a horror movie.
  我不想看恐怖片。
- I don't want to see a movie for children.
  我不想看給小孩子看的電影。

3 The movie is worth seeing. 這部電影值得一看。

- The movie is worthy of seeing.
  這部電影值得一看。
- The movie is nothing more than one big yawn.
  這部電影令人哈欠連天。

4 What kinds of movie do you like best? 你最喜歡哪些類型的電影？

- What is your favorite kind of movie?
  你最喜歡哪類電影？

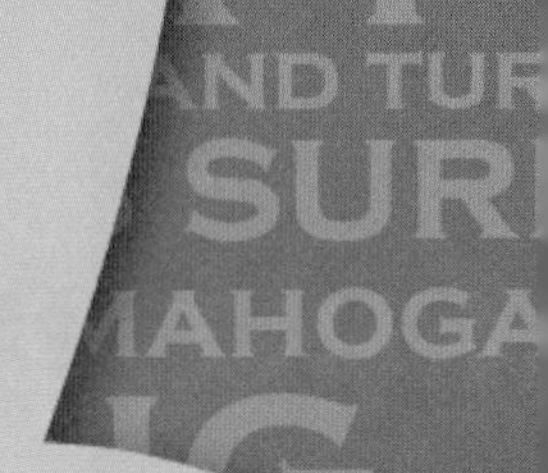

Chapter 9

Feelings
情緒篇

56 Happiness & Misfortune 幸福與不幸

Dialogue 1 第一次聊就上手

track147

Reporter : Congratulations on your lottery!

Chandler : Really? I can't believe it!

Reporter : What do you want to say?

Chandler : I don't know. I'm too happy to say a word.

Reporter : I can understand. It's just like a dream, right?

Chandler : Yes. I'm on cloud nine.

Translation 中譯照過來

記　者：恭喜你中獎了！

錢德勒：真的嗎？我真不敢相信！

記　者：你想說點什麼嗎？

錢德勒：我不知道。我高興的一句話都說不出來了。

記　者：我能理解。就像做夢一樣，是吧？

錢德勒：是的，我感到喜出望外。

Key words 重點單字快速記

happiness [ˋhæpɪnɪs] 名. 快樂，幸福
misfortune [mɪsˋfɔrtʃən] 名. 不幸，厄運
congratulations [kənˏgrætʃəˋleʃənz] 名. 恭喜
lottery [ˋlɑtərɪ] 名. 獎券
dream [drim] 名. 夢

Patterns 延伸句型快速學

01 ***Congratulations on + N.***
（恭喜……。）

> Congratulations on your award.
> 恭喜您獲獎。

02 ***S + be + too + adj. + to V....***
（太……以致於無法……。）

> Edward is too tired to go out.
> 艾德太累了以致於無法出門。

Common Sense 小常識

世界上最幸福的十個國家（1）

根據經濟合作與發展組織（OECD）調查研究，澳洲是世界上最幸福的工業化國家。此次根據健康、教育與技能、環境質量、安全、生活整體滿意度、主觀幸福、社會關係為指標，評估出世界上十大幸福的國家。

1. 澳洲
2. 挪威
3. 瑞典

待續……

56 Happiness & Misfortune 幸福與不幸

Dialogue 2 第一次聊就上手

track148

Monica : Why are you so upset?

Joey : I was fired today.

Monica : Why? You have done a great job.

Joey : But my boss doesn't think so.

Monica : Forget it. You will find a better job.

Joey : Thank you.

Translation 中譯照過來

莫妮卡：你為什麼那麼沮喪？

喬　伊：我今天被炒魷魚了。

莫妮卡：為什麼呢？你做得很好啊。

喬　伊：但我的老闆不這麼認為。

莫妮卡：忘記這些吧，你會找到一份更好的工作的。

喬　伊：謝謝。

Key words 重點單字快速記

upset [ʌp`sɛt] 名. 苦惱的
fired [faɪrd] 動. 被解雇
think [θɪŋk] 動. 思考
forget [fɚ`gɛt] 動. 忘記
better [`bɛtɚ] 形. 更好的

Patterns 延伸句型快速學

01 *S + be + V-ed.*
（某人被……。）

Pitt was killed last week.
比特上週被殺害了。

02 *S + have / has + p.p. + ...*
（某人已經……。）

Nathan has completed his work two hours ago.
奈森兩小時前就已經完成工作了。

Common Sense 小常識

世界上最幸福的十個國家（2）

前述已經看過了最幸福國家前３名，讓我們接著看４～１０名：

4. 丹麥
5. 加拿大
6. 瑞士
7. 美國
8. 芬蘭
9. 荷蘭
10. 紐西蘭

Key Sentences 基本句大變身

track149

1 I'm on cloud nine. 我喜出望外。

- I feel like I'm in heaven.
  我感覺自己進了天堂。
- I'm very happy.
  我非常高興。

2 I'm happy to have such a good friend. 有這樣一個好朋友我很高興。

- I'm happy to be with you.
  跟你在一起我很高興。
- I'm so lucky to married you.
  我真幸運和你結了婚。

3 He is all smiles these days. 他最近老是笑。

- He laughs so often these days.
  這些天他老是笑。
- Her smiling face is just like a flower.
  她的笑臉像花兒一樣。

4 I'm satisfied with the result. 我對這個結果很滿意。

- Are you satisfied with the food?
  你對食物滿意嗎？
- The movie is very satisfying.
  這部電影很令人滿意。

5 Thank you for giving me such a surprise. 謝謝你給了我這樣一個驚喜。

- Thanks for your help.
  感謝你的幫助。
- I'd appreciate for your help.
  我很感激你的幫助。

57 Surprise & Suspicion 驚奇與懷疑

Dialogue 1 第一次聊就上手

track150

Jenny: Hey, how's it going?

Luke: Very bad. I broke my arm yesterday.

Jenny: Is that true? I saw you were fine yesterday.

Luke: Yes, but it happened last night.

Jenny: Really?

Luke: I'm just joking.

Jenny: I knew that!

Translation 中譯照過來

珍妮：嘿，你最近怎麼樣啊？

盧克：很不好。昨天我摔斷了胳膊。

珍妮：真的嗎？昨天我看你還好好的。

盧克：是啊，這是晚上才發生的。

珍妮：你說真的嗎？

盧克：我只是開玩笑的。

珍妮：我就知道！

Chapter1 交際篇
Chapter2 交通運輸篇
Chapter3 用餐事宜篇
Chapter4 愛情篇
Chapter5 校園生活篇
Chapter6 工作篇
Chapter7 購物篇
Chapter8 公共服務篇
Chapter9 情緒篇

Key words 重點單字快速記

surprise [sə`praɪz] 名. 驚奇，驚訝，詫異
suspicion [sə`spɪʃən] 名. 不信任，猜疑
true [tru] 形. 真的，真實的
really [`rɪəlɪ] 副. 真正地
joke [dʒok] 動. 說笑話，開玩笑

Patterns 延伸句型快速學

01 *How's + sth + going?*
（……（進展）怎麼樣？）

> How's your plan going?
> 你的計畫進展得如何？

02 *I saw (that)....*
（我看見……。）

> I saw (that) Kate and Owen had a fight last night.
> 昨晚我看見凱特與歐文在吵架。

Common Sense 小常識

讓美國人驚奇的台灣人習慣（1）

1. 工作擺第一。
2. 凡事愛謙虛。
3. 什麼都敢吃。
4. 愛面子。
5. 沒什麼休閒娛樂。
6. 有話不直說。
7. 愛管閒事。
8. 凡事愛商量。

57 Surprise & Suspicion 驚奇與懷疑

Dialogue 2 第一次聊就上手

track151

Tonny : I'm sorry to be late.

Betty : What's the reason this time?

Tonny : My brother has got a bad cold and I have to take care of him.

Betty : Wasn't he got a cold last week?

Tonny : Are you sure? I thought I said it was my sister.

Betty : I don't think so.

Tonny : Please trust me. My brother is definitely got a cold.

Betty : I don't buy your story.

Translation 中譯照過來

托尼：很抱歉我遲到了。

貝蒂：這次是什麼原因呢？

托尼：我弟弟得了重感冒，我得照顧他。

貝蒂：他上週不是就感冒了嗎？

托尼：你確定？我還以為我說的是我妹妹呢。

貝蒂：我可不這麼認為。

托尼：請相信我，我弟弟真的感冒了。

貝蒂：我才不信呢。

Key words 重點單字快速記

reason [ˋrizn̩] 名. 原因；理由
cold [kold] 名. 感冒
sure [ʃur] 形. 確信的，有把握的
trust [trʌst] 動. 信任，相信
definitely [ˋdɛfənɪtlɪ] 形. 確切地，肯定地

Patterns 延伸句型快速學

01 *I'm sorry to V....*
（我很抱歉（做了）……。）

> I’ m sorry to hear that your grandmother passed away.
> 我很抱歉聽到你的祖母過世了。

02 *Sb + get a (adj.) cold.*
（某人得了感冒。）

> Benson got a cold last weekend.
> 班森上週末感冒了。

Common Sense 小常識

讓美國人驚奇的台灣人習慣（2）

不光是習慣，在文化的方面，西方人也常常驚異於我們的行為，舉凡結了婚還與父母同住、女人生了孩子後必須一個月不洗澡、幼小的孩子必須與父母同睡等……這在他們的眼中是完全不能夠理解的。

Key Sentences 基本句大變身

track152

1 Is that true? 真的嗎？

- Is that real?
  是真的嗎？
- Are you serious?
  你當真的嗎？

2 Are you kidding me? 你是逗我的吧？

- Are you joking?
  你在開玩笑嗎？
- You must be joking.
  你一定是在開玩笑。

3 I don't buy your story. 我才不信呢。

- I know better than that.
  我才不信呢。

4 They haven't much faith in his explanation. 他們不太相信他的解釋。

- Lily hasn't much faith in Jack's promises.
  莉莉不大相信傑克的承諾。

58 Scare & Fear 驚慌與恐懼

Dialogue 1 第一次聊就上手

track153

Alice : Oh, thank God, you're home. I'm so terrified.

Edward : What wrong?

Alice : I think someone was tracking me.

Edward : Do you think we should call the police?

Alice : I'm not sure. But I was falling apart.

Edward : You'd better stay at home these days.

Translation 中譯照過來

愛麗絲：噢，謝天謝地你到家了。我真的很害怕。

愛德華：發生什麼事了？

愛麗絲：我覺得有人跟蹤我了。

愛德華：你覺得我們有必要報警嗎？

愛麗絲：我不確定。但我真的快被嚇死了。

愛德華：你最近最好別出門了。

Key words 重點單字快速記

scare [skɛr] 名. 驚恐，驚嚇
fear [fɪr] 名. 害怕，恐懼
terrified [ˋtɛrə͵faɪd] 形. 非常害怕的，極度驚恐的
track [træk] 動. 追蹤
police [pəˋlis] 名. 警察

Patterns 延伸句型快速學

01 *S + were / was + Ving.*

（某人（過去）正在……。）

> Yang was cleaning the toilet when I talked to the teacher.
> 我跟老師在講話的時候，楊正在掃廁所。

02 *Do you think (that)…?*

（你覺得……嗎？）

> Do you think the answer is wrong?
> 你覺得這個答案是錯的嗎？

Common Sense 小常識

美國最恐怖的瀑布（1）

位於美國明尼蘇達州的「魔鬼水壺」瀑布可以稱得上是美國最恐怖的地方之一了。從外觀上看該瀑布沒有什麼特殊之處，但沒有任何一個人知道這條瀑布通向何處。

待續……

58 Scare & Fear 驚慌與恐懼

Dialogue 2 第一次聊就上手

track154

Damon : Hi, Bonny, what's wrong with you?

Bonny : The scene of this movie is really scary.

Damon : It's just a movie. Don't be afraid.

Bonny : I know. But it's really horrible.

Damon : Then how about going back home to see a comedy?

Bonny : Sounds great!

Translation 中譯照過來

戴蒙：嗨，邦妮，你怎麼了？

邦妮：這部電影的場景太嚇人了。

戴蒙：這只是一部電影，別害怕。

邦妮：我知道，但它真的太恐怖了。

戴蒙：那回家看部喜劇片怎麼樣？

邦妮：好主意！

Key words 重點單字快速記

scene [sin] 名. （電影、書中的）場景，場面
scary [ˋskɛrɪ] 形. 可怕的，駭人的，恐怖的
afraid [əˋfred] 形. 害怕的
horrible [ˋhɔrəbḷ] 形. 可怕的，嚇人的，令人恐懼的
comedy [ˋkɑmədɪ] 名. 喜劇

Patterns 延伸句型快速學

01 *What's wrong with sb / sth?*
（……怎麼了？）

> What's wrong with Mary?
> 瑪莉怎麼了？

02 *Don't be adj. ....*
（別……。）

> Don't be too optimistic about the result.
> 別對結果太樂觀。

Common Sense 小常識

美國最恐怖的瀑布（2）

魔鬼水壺瀑布到底為什麼恐怖呢？它從山體最上方向下流動，到山體中間形成兩個分流，一個支流到山下匯集成河流，比較正常；但另一支在山體一半處流進了一個口朝上的洞穴，這個洞穴永遠填不滿，不管有任何東西掉進去就永遠別想再回來，彷彿無底洞一樣。

Key Sentences 基本句大變身

track155

1 I'm scared of being alone at home. 我害怕一個人在家。

- I'm scared to watch a horror movie.
  我害怕看恐怖電影。
- I'm terrified of taking exams.
  我害怕考試。
- I'm scared to take exams.
  我害怕考試。
- I have a fear of snake.
  我害怕蛇。

2 I'm falling apart. 我要嚇死了。

- I was scared out of my wits.
  我被嚇死了。
- I was frightened to death.
  我被嚇死了。

3 The accident gives me the creeps. 這場事故使我毛骨悚然。

- Snakes give me the shivers.
  蛇讓我毛骨悚然。
- The sight of the accident was horrible.
  那場事故的景象太可怕了。

59 Irritability & Anger 煩躁與生氣

Dialogue 1 第一次聊就上手

track156

Kate : Here you are at last!

Daniel : I'm so sorry for being late.

Kate : I have been waiting for you here for three hours.

Daniel : Please don't be angry. I can explain it.

Kate : Then tell me the reason.

Daniel : My car broke down in the half way, and I couldn't find any taxi, so I had to take a bus....

Kate : Oh, God! Can't you find a better excuse?

Daniel : I'm serious!

Translation 中譯照過來

凱　特：你終於來了！

丹尼爾：真對不起，我遲到了。

凱　特：我在這裡等了你 3 個小時了。

丹尼爾：請別生氣。我可以解釋。

凱　特：那告訴我原因。

丹尼爾：我的車在半路上壞了，我又招不到計程車，所以我只能坐公車來……。

凱　特：噢，天哪！你就不能找個好一點的藉口嗎？

丹尼爾：我是說真的！

Key words 重點單字快速記

irritability [ˌɪrətəˋbɪlətɪ] 名 易怒
anger [ˋæŋgɚ] 名 憤怒，怒火，怒氣
angry [ˋæŋgrɪ] 形 生氣的；憤怒的，發怒的
explain [ɪkˋsplen] 動 解釋
excuse [ɪkˋskjuz] 名 （辯解的）理由；托詞，藉口

Patterns 延伸句型快速學

01 *S + V (+ O) at last.*

（終於……。）

> The plane arrived at last.
> 飛機終於抵達了。

02 *S + have / has been Ving ... + for +* 一段時間 .

（……已經（持續某動作）～（多少時間）了。）

> Upton has been smoking for 20 years.
> 奧普敦已經吸了二十年煙。

Common Sense 小常識

憤怒的美國人（1）

據統計，每年有100多萬美國人需要接受「憤怒管理」課程。尤其是到了購物旺季，這些暴躁的消費者總是要逼得美國商場動用憤怒管理專家來安撫他們，聽起來是不是很不可思議？！

59 Irritability & Anger 煩躁與生氣

Dialogue 2 第一次聊就上手

track157

Jim : My boss is so boresome that I want to resign.

Lily : Why?

Jim : He always makes me work overtime. I really can't stand this!

Lily : I can understand. Let's forget it and have some fun!

Jim : You're right.

Translation 中譯照過來

吉姆：我的老闆太煩人了，我想辭職不幹了。

莉莉：為什麼呢？

吉姆：他總是讓我加班。我真的無法忍受了！

莉莉：我能理解。讓我們忘了這件事，痛快玩一會兒吧！

吉姆：你說得對。

Key words 重點單字快速記

boresome [ˋborsəm] 形. 令人厭煩的；無聊的
resign [rɪˋzaɪn] 動. 辭（職），放棄（工作或職位）
overtime [ˏovɚˋtaɪm] 動. 使超過時間
stand [stænd] 動. 接受；忍受
fun [fʌn] 名. 樂趣

Patterns 延伸句型快速學

01 ***so adj. that S + V....***
（太……以致於……。）

The cake is so sweet that some people hate it.
蛋糕太甜了以致於有些人討厭它。

02 ***make + sb + V.***
（使某人去做某事。）

My wife makes me wash the toilet every week.
我老婆要我每週都去洗廁所。

Common Sense 小常識

憤怒的美國人（2）

根據維吉尼亞州，林奇堡市的憤怒化解研究所主任道爾．金特里博士統計，美國人平均每人每週要發怒兩次，其中女人發怒時間較長，而男人發怒的強度較大。

Key 基本句大變身 Sentences

track158

1 I really hate waiting here. 我真的很討厭在這裡空等。

- I'm really angry about waiting here.
  在這裡等待真的讓我很生氣。

2 I'm really angry about his words. 他的話實在讓我生氣。

- Their rudeness really burns me up.
  他們的無禮真讓我生氣。
- He got my blood up by criticizing my best friend.
  他批評我朋友讓我很生氣。

3 I can't bear the way he talks. 我無法忍受他說話的方式。

- I can't stand to talk with him.
  我不能忍受跟他談話。
- I am getting impatient with you doing this all the time.
  我不能忍受你老是這樣做。

4 I'm fed up with his bad temper. 我受夠了他的壞脾氣。

- I'm fed up with his bad behavior.
  我受夠了他的壞行為。
- I've had enough of your insolence, and I'm having no more.
  我受夠了你的傲慢，我不能再忍了。

60 Hope & Disappointment 希望與失望

Dialogue 1 第一次聊就上手

track159

John : I hope it will be a sunny day tomorrow.

Lisa : So what?

John : So we can have a picnic together.

Lisa : That's a great idea, but I'm afraid you will be disappointed.

John : Why?

Lisa : I heard from the weather forecast that it's going to rain tomorrow.

John : What a pity!

Translation 中譯照過來

約翰：希望明天是個晴天。

莉薩：那又如何？

約翰：那樣我們就可以一起去野餐了。

莉薩：好主意！但恐怕你要失望了。

約翰：為什麼？

莉薩：我聽天氣預報說明天會下雨。

約翰：好可惜！

Key words 重點單字快速記

hope [hop] 動. 希望，期望
sunny [ˋsʌnɪ] 形. 充滿陽光的
disappointment [ˏdɪsəˋpɔɪntmənt] 名. 失望，掃興
disappointed [ˏdɪsəˋpɔɪntɪd] 形. 失望的，沮喪的
pity [ˋpɪtɪ] 名. 可惜，遺憾

Patterns 延伸句型快速學

01 *I hope (that) ....*

（（我）希望……。）

I hope that I can pass my calculus exam with flying colors.
我希望我能以優異的成績通過我的微積分考試。

02 *What + a + N.*

（多……啊！）

What a wonderful day!
多麼好的一天啊！

Common Sense 小常識

美國人的願望（1）

與台灣不同，對美國人來說，買房子根本算不上是一件難事，那麼美國人究竟有什麼願望呢？

* 減肥
* 有計劃的生活
* 存錢
* 享受生活
* 健身

60 Hope & Disappointment 希望與失望

Dialogue 2 第一次聊就上手

track160

Manager : Can I talk with you?

Joey : Sure. What is it?

Manager : I am disappointed with your work performance these days.

Joey : Why?

Manager : The progress of your project is so slow.

Joey : Well, I'm sorry. There are some problems in my family. I promise I will focus on my work.

Manager : OK, don't let me down.

Translation 中譯照過來

經理：能和你談談嗎？

喬伊：當然可以。有什麼事嗎？

經理：我對你這幾天的工作表現很失望。

喬伊：為什麼？

經理：你的專案進展太慢了。

喬伊：嗯，對不起。我家裡最近發生了一些事。但我保證會把精力都放在工作上的。

經理：好吧，別讓我失望。

Key words 重點單字快速記

performance [pɚˋfɔrməns] 名. （工作或活動中的）表現
progress [prəˋgrɛs] 動. 前進
project [ˋprɑdʒɛkt] 名. 專案
slow [slo] 形. 緩慢的
problem [ˋprɑbləm] 名. 問題

Patterns 延伸句型快速學

01 *I promise (that) ....*

（我保證……。）

> I promise that my team will go back to the training after the party.
> 我保證我的隊伍會在派對後回去練習。

02 *... let sb down.*

（……讓某人失望。）

> Henry lets his father down for failing the qualification.
> 亨利因沒通過資格考試而讓他父親失望。

Common Sense 小常識

美國人的願望（2）

前面看過了一些美國人的願望，下面再來看一些其他的吧：

* 學習一些有趣的東西
* 戒煙
* 幫助他人實現願望
* 遇到相愛的人
* 多與家人在一起

Key Sentences 基本句大變身

track161

1 I hope I can pass the exam. 我希望我能通過考試。

- I hope it will rain tomorrow.
  我希望明天會下雨。
- Here's hoping that I can pass the exam.
  希望我能通過考試。

2 I'm disappointed at the result. 我對結果很失望。

- I was disappointed that I didn't pass the exam.
  沒能通過考試我感到很失望。
- The cancellation of the game was a real letdown.
  比賽取消真是令人失望。

3 The result could have been better. 結果原本可以更好的。

- The show could have been better.
  這個表演本來可以更好的。
- I was more disappointed than discouraged.
  我的失望大於洩氣。

61 Concern & Anxiety 擔心與憂慮

Dialogue 1 第一次聊就上手

track162

Jim: What's the matter?

Lucy: I'm in a flap about the exam.

Jim: Please relax. Our professor is not so strict.

Lucy: I hope so.

Jim: I think you can do a great job at the final exam.

Lucy: I have to, or I won't be able to pass the course.

Translation 中譯照過來

吉姆：怎麼了？

露西：我為考試感到慌張。

吉姆：請放輕鬆。我們的教授沒有那麼嚴格。

露西：希望如此。

吉姆：我覺得你期末考試可以考得很好。

露西：我必須要考好，不然我就要被當了。

Key words 重點單字快速記

concern [kən`sɝn] 名 憂慮，擔心，關切
動 使憂慮，使擔心
anxiety [æŋ`zaɪətɪ] 名 不安，擔心，焦慮
flap [flæp] 名 慌亂；激動；焦急
relax [rɪ`læks] 動 放鬆
professor [prə`fɛsɚ] 名 教授

Patterns 延伸句型快速學

01 ***..., or ....***
（……，不然／否則……。）

I have to get home in time, or my wife is going to kill me.
我必須準時回家，否則我老婆會殺了我。

02 ***S + be able to + V.***
（……可以／能（做）……。）

Will is able to do 100 push-ups at a time.
威爾能一次做 100 個伏地挺身。

Common Sense 小常識

焦慮的美國人（1）

在美國，有近五分之一的人都患有焦慮症，他們花在抗焦慮藥物上的錢已經達到了每年 20 億美元，大約相當於 600 億元台幣，真的非常驚人！

61 Concern & Anxiety 擔心與憂慮

Dialogue 2 第一次聊就上手

track163

Emily : What's wrong with you? You look so nervous.

Jack : I am going to New York by plane.

Emily : So what makes you anxious?

Jack : You know, there have been several air crashes in the news recently.

Emily : Don't worry. That's just accidents.

Jack : Well, but it still can happen, right?

Translation 中譯照過來

艾米麗：怎麼了？你看起來很緊張。

傑　克：我要坐飛機去紐約。

艾米麗：那什麼事讓你那麼擔心呢？

傑　克：你知道的，最近新聞上說有幾起空難事件。

艾米麗：別擔心，那只是意外。

傑　克：好吧，但依然可能發生，不是嗎？

Key words 重點單字快速記

nervous [ˋnɝvəs] 形. 神經緊張的；焦慮不安的
plane [plen] 名. 飛機
anxious [ˋæŋkʃəs] 形. 焦慮的，不安的，擔心的
recently [ˋrisn̩tlɪ] 副. 近來
accident [ˋæksədənt] 名. 意外

Patterns 延伸句型快速學

01 ***by*** **+ 交通工具 .**
（搭乘……。）

> We are going to San Francisco by train.
> 我們要搭火車去舊金山。

02 ***S + V (+ O), right?***
（……，不是嗎？）

> He is Jenny's brother, right?
> 他是珍妮的弟弟，不是嗎？

Common Sense 小常識

焦慮的美國人（2）

在世界心理健康調查 (World Mental Health Survey) 計畫的 14 個國家中，美國人被認為是最焦慮的族群，其達到顯著臨床水準的人數甚至比奈及利亞、黎巴嫩和烏克蘭還多。

Key Sentences 基本句大變身

track164

1 I'm in a flap about the exam. 考試讓我覺得十分慌張。

- I'm in a flap about the speech.
  我對演講感到緊張不已。
- I was in a fluster at the thought of meeting the boss.
  一想到要見老闆，我就緊張。
- I feel nervous about the result of the contest.
  我為比賽結果感到緊張不安。
- I'm worrying about the result of the contest.
  我很擔心比賽結果。

2 I fear for the result of the operation. 我擔心手術的結果。

- I fear that it may cause an accident.
  我擔心它可能會引起事故。
- I'm concerned about my sister's health condition.
  我擔心我妹妹的健康狀況。
- I'm concerned that it may not work.
  我擔心它可能不起作用。

62 Nit-picking & Blame 挑剔與埋怨

Dialogue 1 第一次聊就上手

track165

Husband : Would you please stop doing that?

Wife : What's wrong?

Husband : Stop keeping tapping your pen on the desk. It's driving me crazy.

Wife : OK. Fine! Would you mind not slurping when you eat?

Husband : Oh, come on. How can you hear that when you're shouting into your phone?

Translation 中譯照過來

丈夫：你能不能別再那樣做了？

妻子：怎麼了？

丈夫：別再用筆敲桌子了，都快把我逼瘋了。

妻子：好啊！那你吃東西的時候也別再發出聲音了好嗎？

丈夫：噢，得了吧！你一直對著電話喊的時候，怎麼可能聽得見呢？

Key words 重點單字快速記

blame [blem] 名. 責備
tap [tæp] 動. （用手指）輕拍，輕叩，輕敲
drive [draɪv] 動. 迫使，促使（某人做某事）
crazy [ˋkrezɪ] 形. 生氣的；煩惱的
slurp [slɝp] 動. 出聲地喝（水等）

Patterns 延伸句型快速學

01 ***Would you stop + Ving ...?***
（你能停止做……嗎？）

Would you stop kicking my chair?
你能不能不要再踢我的椅子了？

02 ***Would you mind (not) Ving ...?***
（你能（別）做……嗎？）

Would you mind opening the window for me?
你能幫我開窗嗎？

Common Sense 小常識

挑剔的美國人

東方人在表達上較為含蓄，相對而言美國人則比較直接，對於喜歡的人和事物，他們會毫不吝嗇地表達出自己的喜愛之情。

Chapter1 交際篇
Chapter2 交通運輸篇
Chapter3 用餐事宜篇
Chapter4 愛情篇
Chapter5 校園生活篇
Chapter6 工作篇
Chapter7 購物篇
Chapter8 公共服務篇
Chapter9 情緒篇

62 Nit-picking & Blame 挑剔與埋怨

Dialogue 2 第一次聊就上手

track166

Jenny : I need to complain.

Postal clerk : What's wrong?

Jenny : Your delivery staff was late for three hours this morning.

Postal clerk : I'm so sorry to hear that.

Jenny : It makes me late for work today.

Postal clerk : I apologize for that and we will give the postage back to you.

Translation 中譯照過來

珍　　妮：我要投訴！

郵局職員：出了什麼問題？

珍　　妮：你們的送貨員今天上午晚來了 3 個小時。

郵局職員：聽到這個我很抱歉。

珍　　妮：因為這個，我今天上班都遲到了。

郵局職員：我為這個道歉，我們會把郵資退還給您的。

Key words 重點單字快速記

complain [kəm`plen] 動. 抱怨，不滿，發牢騷
delivery [dɪ`lɪvərɪ] 名. 傳送
staff [stæf] 名. 員工
apologize [ə`pɑlə͵dʒaɪz] 動. 道歉
postage [`postɪdʒ] 名. 郵資

Patterns 延伸句型快速學

01 ***S + be late for +*** 一段時間 ***.***
（……晚了（多久）。）

The shipping was late for four days.
送貨晚了四天才抵達。

02 ***I apologize for N / Ving....***
（我為……感到很抱歉。）

I apologize for telling the lie.
我為說謊道歉。

Common Sense 小常識

挑剔的美國人

美國人對於不喜歡的事物到底有多麼的直接呢？舉個例子來說，面對不感興趣的人或事時，他們或許會直接說一句"That sucks"，意思是「太爛了，太糟了，太差勁了」。

Key Sentences 基本句大變身

track167

1	Could you hurry up?	你可以快一點嗎？

- Can't you be a bit quicker? 你就不能快點嗎？
- Can you bustle the children up? 你能催孩子們快一點嗎？

2	I need to complain of the product.	我需要投訴一下這件產品。

- I have a complaint about the product. 我要說說這件產品的事。
- I'm phoning to complain about the product. 我打電話來投訴產品。

3	I'm sorry to say this, but the product doesn't work.	很抱歉這樣說，但這產品不能用。

- I'm sorry to say it doesn't work. 很遺憾，它並不起作用。
- It didn't do a smite of good. 一點效果也沒有。

4	Do you have to open the window?	你就一定要把窗戶打開嗎？

- Do you have to shout like this? 難道你一定要這樣大喊大叫嗎？
- Have you got to leave so soon? 你一定要這麼早離開嗎？

5	Would you please not talk like that?	請你別那樣說話好嗎？

- Would you please not smoke here? 請你別在這兒抽煙好嗎？
- Please don't slam the door. 請不要使勁關門。

語研力 E024

臨時需要的一句話！用聊天學英文句型，3 秒就學會

大腦建構句型藍圖，英文脫口說更容易！

作　　者　優尼創新外語研發中心◎編著
顧　　問　曾文旭
總 編 輯　黃若璇
編輯總監　耿文國
美術編輯　李澤恩、王晴葳
文字校對　林旻豫、蘇麗娟
音檔校對　林旻豫
法律顧問　北辰著作權事務所

印　　製　世和印製企業有限公司
初　　版　2018 年 7 月
（本書為《第一次用英語聊天，超簡單！》之修訂版）
出　　版　凱信企業集團 - 凱信企業管理顧問有限公司
電　　話　（02）2752-5618
傳　　真　（02）2752-5619
地　　址　106 台北市大安區忠孝東路四段 250 號 11 樓之 1

定　　價　新台幣 299 元 / 港幣 100 元
產品內容　1 書 + 1 MP3

總 經 銷　商流文化事業有限公司
地　　址　235 新北市中和區中正路 752 號 8 樓
電　　話　（02）2228-8841
傳　　真　（02）2228-6939

港澳地區總經銷　和平圖書有限公司
地　　址　香港柴灣嘉業街 12 號百樂門大廈 17 樓
電　　話　（852）2804-6687
傳　　真　（852）2804-6409

國家圖書館出版品預行編目資料

臨時需要的一句話！用聊天學英文句型，3 秒就學會 / 優尼創新外語研發中心編著 .
-- 初版 . -- 臺北市：凱信企管顧問 , 2018.07
面；　公分
ISBN 978-986-9628-04-4 (平裝附光碟片)

1. 英語 2. 句法
805.169　　107010499

用對的方法充實自己，
讓人生變得更美好！

凱信企管

用對的方法充實自己，
讓人生變得更美好！